GRANTA BOOKS

HARP

JOHN GREGORY DUNNE

Harp

GRANTA BOOKS

CAMBRIDGE

in association with
PENGUIN BOOKS

GRANTA BOOKS
44a Hobson Street, Cambridge CB1 1NL

Published in association with the Penguin Group
27 Wrights Lane, London W8 5TZ, England
Viking Penguin Inc., 40 West 23rd Street, New York, NY 10010, USA
Penguin Books Australia Ltd, Ringwood, Victoria, Australia
Penguin Books Canada Ltd, 2801 John Street,
Markham, Ontario, Canada L3R 1B4
Penguin Books (NZ) Ltd, 182–190 Wairau Road,
Auckland 10, New Zealand

Penguin Books Ltd, Registered Offices: Harmondsworth,
Middlesex, England

First published in the USA by Simon & Schuster Inc. 1989
First published in Great Britain by Granta Books 1990
1 3 5 7 9 10 8 6 4 2

Made and printed in Great Britain by
Butler & Tanner, Frome and London

A CIP catalogue record for this book is available from the British Library

ISBN 0-14-014210-X

This book is for my friend Tony Richardson
It is for my friends Alan and Marilyn Bergman
And finally it is for dearest of the dear Laure Dunne
And her sons Harrison, Justin and Evan

Try to be one of the people on whom
nothing is lost.

—HENRY JAMES

When Irish eyes are smiling
Sure it's like a morn in spring.
In the lilt of Irish laughter
You can hear the angels sing. . . .

—OLD IRISH LIE

I was not given to personal reflection, had always looked unkindly, in fact, on introspection. Then in the seventh year of the Reagan kakistocracy, the medical dyes shooting through my arterial freeways were forced to make a detour around a major obstruction:

PART ONE

I

THERE IS no good that can come from a telephone call at 4:30 in the morning. The best you can hope for is a wrong number, a drunken friend, a hang-up. I looked at the luminous bright blue figures on the digital clock radio and I hoped it was a dream and I hoped the ringing would stop and when it didn't I ran over the possibilities as I reached, still drugged with sleep, for the receiver—my daughter, on a school camping trip to Yosemite (sweet Jesus! the thought nearly stayed my hand), my aunt, the last family survivor of her generation, vital, exasperating, still a force, but after all eighty-three years old. Not Stephen, never Stephen, Stephen in the white sailor suit, Stephen with hair the color of sunlight, Stephen the baby of the family, Stephen my brother, Stephen the husband and father, Stephen the graphics designer, Stephen who had the gift of laughter, Stephen, at forty-three, dead of his own hand, a suicide.

It is an imposition on the reader to write that paragraph, but there are those of us for whom words have no meaning until they are down on paper. Clarity only comes when pen is in hand, or at the typewriter or the word processor, clarity about what we feel and what we think, how we love and how we mourn; the words on the page constitute the benediction, the declaration, the confession of the emotionally inarticulate. I do not wish to eulogize Stephen; he was far too private, and even the wish would embarrass him. Nor will I try to understand him; it is hubris of an almost obscene dimension to pretend that one person can ever truly understand another.

I only wish to remember him. I sit in an office surrounded by fragments of his life and mine, old photographs taken in houses I no longer remember, crumbling newspaper clippings of graduations and engagements and weddings, scribbled notes with references to people only dimly recalled, pictures of aunts and uncles and second cousins of another generation, mass cards printed for the funerals of each of our parents, snapshots of old girlfriends of his and a former fiancée of mine, a proposal for a graphics design corporation that Stephen planned to start and I invest in, Christmas cards from Stephen and Laure with first one son and then a second and then a third. Each memento is a shard of memory, a tile in a mosaic that reveals all and tells nothing. There is Stephen in a playpen and there I am in what appears to be a Royal Canadian Mountie costume: was it Stephen who called me "Sheriff"? It had the touch of his irony.

Our father was a surgeon, our mother a housewife; my father's parents died before I was born, and I can never remember their given names, nor my paternal grandmother's maiden name; they had no role in our lives. There were six children in our family, and we divided into the Four Oldest and the Two Youngest; Stephen and I were the youngest, thrown together by the divisions of age, and we became as close as tree and bark. Our family was Irish and Catholic on both sides, and we carried a full cargo of ethnic and religious freight as it shifted in the long passage between immigration and deracination. There were times in my life when I, unlike Stephen, tried to disavow the Irish and the Catholic, an effort that was always a source of amusement to him. Stephen had perfect pitch for pretension, especially mine, and a cold eye for the warts and wens of social nuance. Until I went away to college, we shared a room at home, and for a period in New York until I got married we shared an apartment.

The last time I saw him, two or three months before he died, he reminded me that when we were children he would often do my crying for me. Our father was a quick man with a strap to enforce discipline; it was a matter of pride with me not to cry. Indeed I would start to giggle when I returned to our room, and Stephen, fearful that my father would give me another taste of the leather, would keen loudly to avert that possibility. We both had a tendency to stammer, and whenever we met, all too rarely the last fifteen years of his life, we would discuss stratagems to avoid the minefields of speech. I used to say "howdy" because I would stumble on "hello," and he would say "wee" because he would falter on "little," and when we compared tactics we would dissolve in laughter, a laughter that only another stammerer could ever understand. From childhood on, Stephen could make me laugh. I remember a golden-haired four-year-old, in a perfect fury at being banished from a family dinner for my sister's violin teacher when there was no room at the table, poking his towhead into the dining room and saying the dirtiest thing he could imagine: "Hey, kids, enema tube."

We spoke often on the telephone when my wife and I moved to California, and saw each other whenever we were in the East. He was best man at my wedding and I at his; he was my daughter's godfather and I godfather to his eldest son.

That wise woman my mother would often tell me that Stephen played life on the dark keys, but I never heard the melody. I did not know that for years there were intermittent bouts of melancholy, dark downward spirals. Once in a while we talked about depression, but in the way one talked about fevers now safely passed, viruses isolated and inoculated against. I called them "the jits," head colds of the psyche. We even devised a cure: bed rest, Heath bars and Oreo cookies. The following Christmas Stephen's present to me was a perfectly printed five-color photograph of a glass of milk and a stack of Oreos. I was impatient with the emotional extortion of much of what passed for depression. I thought it a bid for attention, a demand for a close-up on the soundstage of life. I had a routine on this sort of theatrics, and the last time I saw Stephen I did my performance and he threw me lines from the wings, and we laughed—oh, God, how we laughed. It was not in Stephen's nature to do a star turn, to give his melancholy billing. What I saw in Stephen was always the same thing: someone I was always truly happy to see. Sometimes when we were alone we would speculate on which one of the six children would die first. Never Stephen, never I; we always settled on one of the others. And then the telephone rang at 4:30 in the morning. He had gone into his garage and with infinite care taped the doors and windows shut. Then he got into his car, started the engine and asphyxiated himself.

THERE ARE things to do when there is a sudden death, and the first thing I did, I did badly. I called one of my two older brothers, a motion picture and television producer, who had come upon bad times of his own, an almost terminal crisis of confidence. He was living in a small cottage in a rural Oregon community, trying to piece his life back together. It took some time to reach him—he had no direct telephone—and when I told him what had happened, there was a cry of such bleakness that I can remember it still. He pulled himself together and said he had been contemplating suicide himself, perhaps even at the exact same moment as Stephen; it was as if the nature of Stephen's death had foreclosed an option. It was then I added quite unnecessarily that there was no need for him to go back to the funeral—he had not really known Stephen all that well, I said, Stephen being ten years younger— and in any event I could not afford to pay his way east. I blame neither the stress of the situation nor my reaction to it for saying something he quite rightly thought wanton and insensitive. We had not, in fact, got along in years, which was more to the point. The reasons for what at times was a quite active, and often quite poisonous, mutual dislike I think are best attributed to, if I may paraphrase Alexander Pope, that long disease, life. Our war was not so much cold as gelid; in seasons of détente we were correct. He had gone to Oregon in search of an epiphany, and from there I was the occasional recipient of long, artful letters, full of character evaluation and private secrets and revisionist family history; blame was sprinkled like holy water; the archbishop of this schismatic church was careful to douse himself as well as his congregation of family. I had the uneasy feeling that there was an audience for this exchange of letters to which I was not privy, with the result that my answers became at best perfunctory. Some weeks after Stephen died, my wife read his next letter but I refused; it appeared more or less a compendium of my shortcomings in most of the moral arenas, beginning with my telephone call that terrible morning. I threw it into the fire, unread; fair enough, but instead of letting it go at that, I was impelled to announce I had done so in a brief communiqué to Oregon, I who had claimed to Stephen, that last time we saw each other, that I had little interest in the theater of my own life, and none whatsoever in the theater of anyone else's; these are the small self-deceptions by which we are defined. "Fuck you," came back the immediate and spontaneous reply; my note, he said, had been much discussed at his support group, which at least confirmed my suspicion that ours had not been a private correspondence.

OF THE REST of that day Stephen died I remember only the logistics. Before Joan—my wife—and I left for the East, I had to make a codicil to my will; my daughter was a minor and Stephen was designated her guardian in the event Joan and I died in what lawyers call, in their insensitivity to the meaning of words, "a mutual disaster," and the round-trip plane flight, for someone as fearful of flying as I, presented two such opportunities. I got hold of my lawyer and he dictated the language I needed for a letter to be left on my desk, with a copy mailed to him, appointing another guardian in the event of an accident. I was especially conditioned to this possibility because for years I had been playing with a story about a suicide that brought a family together for a funeral. Except that the plane bringing one of the siblings had crashed, and the funeral had become instead of an occasion of mourning a battleground of recriminations.

Then there was the problem of my Aunt Harriet Burns in Hartford, my family home, the place where we all had grown up and where my oldest brother and my two sisters still lived. Aunt Harriet was the family matriarch, the last survivor of my parents' generation. She was what used to be called a spinster, briefly in her twenties a nun, a daily communicant sustained in her Catholic faith, or so the family thought, by the most stringent interpretation of the Ten Commandments. My two sisters, fearing how she might react to the fact of Stephen's suicide and to what she might regard as its affront to God and the Church, had told her he had died of a heart attack. They had always, I think, underestimated her capacity for absorbing the untenable. She was rarely given the whole truth, as old people so seldom are by their children or next of kin. When Stephen's wife—widow now—learned what Aunt Harriet had been told, she called me in Los Angeles just as we were leaving for the flight to Hartford (we were to drive to Stephen's house outside New York the next day) and deputized me to tell her what had really happened. (My two brothers could not get flights until the following day.) And so I flew across the country with that additional burden.

We arrived in Hartford late in the evening. There were a number of people in Aunt Harriet's house—Stephen's oldest friend, my two sisters and their husbands, Aunt Harriet. She was sitting in what she and my mother called the family room, a description I always hated, perhaps because it suggested not any family I knew but the idealized family of my mother's wishes. My sister Harriet had recently had a mastectomy—she was to die of cancer a year almost to the day later—and to lighten the mood I made a forced joke about which breast had been removed. My sisters wanted to know how I was going to tell Aunt Harriet. I said I did not know, I just wanted everyone to clear out of the house, I did not want an audience, I wanted to be alone with just her and my wife. Reluctantly they all finally straggled out.

There was a footstool next to Aunt Harriet's chair, and there I sat, at her feet. I knew she did not believe the story about the heart attack, that she intuited blank spaces in the account she had been given. "Aunt Harriet," I said, brutally to the point, "Stephen killed himself." She stared at me, then her head sank to her chest, and for a moment—just a moment—she wept. She composed herself almost immediately, and listened as I described the circumstances of Stephen's death. "You have to think of it the same way you think of cancer," I said. "Or heart disease. It was a malignant disease of the mind." I need not have worried about her reaction. "You know, he can be buried in the Church," she said. I had not known that, the result of not having been a practicing Catholic for thirty years; I still thought the Church refused a suicide mass and burial in sacred ground.

Stephen had a funeral mass with all the trimmings. The priest who had christened him nearly forty-four years earlier delivered the homily. I had hired a car and a driver and we left for New York and our flight back to Los Angeles a few hours after the service. On the ride to the airport there was one terrible moment. I started to doze in the back seat, and suddenly, just before I fell asleep, I fought myself awake. I wondered, and wonder still, if poor Stephen, dear Stephen, had one last moment like that, one moment when he realized he was slipping away, one moment when he wanted it all back.

I TRIED, in those weeks after Stephen's funeral, to comprehend what happened. I looked at the old photographs, I looked at the jacket he designed for my second book, I looked at the tart letter he wrote to a friend of mine who had stiffed him for the fee on a record jacket. I finally concluded that it was presumptuous and self-serving to look for an answer, to think that I or anyone could have stopped him from keeping a date he had made long before. On my desk I kept a copy of the poems of Gerard Manley Hopkins, and it was this poetry that I read, almost obsessively, after Stephen died.

> O the mind, mind has mountains, cliffs of fall,
> Frightful, sheer, no man fathomed. Hold
> Them cheap
> May who ne'er hung there . . .

From another stanza:

> I wake and feel the fell of dark, not day . . .

It is a line filled with terror, a terror I hate to think that Stephen felt. And then:

> I have desired to go
> Where springs not fail,
> To fields where flies no sharp and sided hail
> And a few lilies blow.

I remember spending Christmas in Hartford a year or so before Stephen died. An acquaintance of the family had committed suicide the day after Christmas. Ever the optimist, Aunt Harriet had said, "Well, at least he didn't ruin their Christmas." Stephen looked at me, a cigarette burning his finger, a smile softening the corner of his face. "No," he said, "but he sure tore the shit out of their December twenty-sixth." I think of Stephen and I know there will be a small piece torn out of every day for the rest of my days. I will not ask why. I hold his mountains dear. I hope he is where the lilies blow.

II

What I can never forget, when I sit down to write, is that I am someone born in my age, subject to its pressures, prejudices and expectations, scorched by its past, living in its present. . . .

—PAUL SCOTT

IN GENERAL, it is bad business for a writer to talk about writing. In general, I agree with William Faulkner, who once said that a writer's obituary should read, "He wrote the books, then he died." Faulkner, of course, was given to remarks like that. My favorite is the reason he gave for declining an invitation to dine at the White House with John and Jacqueline Kennedy: "It's a long way to go for dinner." Allowing for the Faulkner caveat, I would like to state a few basic facts. I am a writer. I am a professional writer. I write to make a living. If writing is my calling, it is also my job, the same way that medicine is both a doctor's calling and his job. It is the only job I have. I do not teach, I rarely lecture. I occasionally do screenplays,

24

but the operative word is "do"; doing screenplays does for me what doing screenplays did for Faulkner: it buys time.

The English critic Walter Allen once postulated that the writer is a permanent child. "Part of the impulse that drives the novelist to make his imitation world," Allen wrote in *The English Novel*, "must always be the sheer delight in his own skill in making it. Part of the time he is, as it were, taking the observed universe to pieces, and assembling it again for the simple and naive pleasure of doing so. He can no more help playing than a child can." To this childlike pleasure in the act of writing I would like to add a childlike curiosity. Writing in fact is a license to be curious. I, for example, am interested in how things work, in how a creative movie deal is structured, how a conglomerate is formed. How a tooth is reconstructed or an aorta patched. How a geologist pinpoints a possible oil strike, how an immunologist isolates a virus. How a fire investigator knows when a fire is an accident and when because of the pattern of smoke stains in the burnt-out shell and the sponginess of the floor it is arson. How a pathologist knows that the prostate is the last male organ and the uterus the last female organ destroyed in a fire, how carbon granules in the bronchial passages indicate the victim was alive when the fire started and fat globules in the lung tissue mean that the victim was attacked before the fire. How Fernando Valenzuela throws a screwball, how the air currents and the speed of the projectile and the angle of the wrist at the point of release conspire to make a pitch man was not intended to throw nor his elbow to endure.

This curiosity inexorably draws the writer to his own past. If a writer does not respond to his own past—never mind that he may not understand it—then I suspect he can never be a very good writer. No matter what the writer is writing about, no matter where his curiosity takes him, he is always essentially investigating himself, he is always trying to reprogram the responses to his own history.

I AM A HARP, that is my history, Irish and Catholic, from steerage to suburbia in three generations. The Kennedys defined a certain kind of Irish: Don't get mad, get even, was the commandment to which they swore allegiance—Irish to be sure, but gentrified. I am cut from a rougher bolt of Irish cloth: Get mad *and* get even is the motto on the standard I fly. I call myself a harp because I like the sound of the word—it is short, sharp and abusive. Christopher Isherwood once told me that he preferred being called a faggot to being called gay; words like faggot and kike and nigger, Christopher said, were simple and unequivocal, and the person who called himself the one that fit defined his attitude toward the world.

In the New England where I grew up, being Irish and Catholic meant being a social outcast. This was in the years before John Kennedy was elected president in 1960, an event that, difficult as it is to believe now, offered to certain sections of New England a kind of absolution for having a tainted ethnic and religious pedigree. With a distaste not allayed by my years, I still call Hartford Protestants "Yanks"; WASP belongs to the sanitized diction of pop anthropology. The Irish Catholics of my parents' generation did not know Protestants. They did not know Jews, let alone blacks. In a surfeit of Yank good humor, Whetten Road in West Hartford, where the richest Jewish families lived, was called, by Protestant gentry and upwardly mobile harps alike, Kikes Peak. When my wife and I were married, in the mid-1960s, my mother gave a reception for us in Hartford. There were 125 people present;

124 were Irish Catholics; the 125th was my wife, who was an Episcopalian and—worse—a Californian.

In this Irish diaspora, there was a whole set of unwritten rules, a survival kit, as it were, for the interloper in the Yank jungle. Paramount among the rules was the injunction "Don't make waves." Aunt Harriet would tell me not to make waves, and my mother, especially after my father died, she a widow charged with the upbringing of six children, five still to be educated. Don't make waves meant know your place, don't stand out so that the Yanks could see you, don't let your pretensions became a focus of Yank merriment and mockery. Not making waves offered the possibility of Yank acceptance. Yank norms were the approved norms; risk-taking in areas beyond the traditional ways of making a living invited disapproval; risk-taking made waves. "It never hurts to have a friend in court," was another diaspora aphorism; it was of course implicit that the friend was a Yank, who would be judicious if waves were not made. To those who chose to wander outside the established Irish pecking order, it was asked, "What's so good about you?" It never seemed to occur to the diaspora Irish that playing the Yanks' game only encouraged a servant mentality, one laced with a sour envy, and worse, one that made lives of caution and contented mediocrity attractive.

My parents' generation of course did not see it that way. My mother was only forty-eight when my father died (actually forty-nine; until her last illness she always took one year off her age, a white lie she did not admit until she prepared to meet her maker), and I don't think it ever occurred to her to remarry; widowhood, the widow business, was part of God's plan, and to interfere was blasphemy. She was a hard woman with whom to argue the social logic that gave order to her life, tough and smart, but born and forever a daughter of the diaspora. She had a sharp temper and a sharper tongue, and when I was a child she could deliver a sudden stinging slap on the face that effectively stamped out adolescent rebellion. Into my early middle age, she would listen to some heresy I would put forth, and when I finished, she would pause, collect her thoughts, and finally, inevitably, curtail argument with the same four words, "Your breath is bad," a response that even as I remember it can still infuriate. "What's the matter with the good old middle?" she liked to ask when some social risk was in order, and it would pain me to hear her say it. If she ever read a word I wrote, she was circumspect about mentioning it. A writer made waves, and I wrote about the Irish and sex, and those were subjects that in her mind did not just make waves, they made a fucking typhoon.

The summer after my father's death, my mother and my Aunt Harriet were swindled—there is no other word for it— out of a great deal of money by a harp sharpie in collusion with the directors of one of Hartford's larger banks. Here was the situation: Do—my mother's name was Dorothy, and after I left home I always called her Do, pronounced "doe," as all her friends did—and Aunt Harriet were the two largest stock-holders in the bank my grandfather—they and we always called him Poppa—had founded. That summer, just weeks after my father died, Poppa's bank was set to merge with an-other Hartford bank, a Yank stronghold. The merger conver-sations were secret, and it was under the prevailing secrecy that my mother was approached by an officer in Poppa's bank with a proposal: that she and my aunt sell a large portion of their shares back to the new entity so that their combined holdings would not dominate the bank that would emerge from the merger. It was further suggested that if they did not agree, if two "women" held so many shares, the merger might not go through. (Not just two women, I always thought, but two Catholic women.) They were also told that under no circumstances were they to repeat the burden of the conversation either to their lawyer or to their accountant. Do and Aunt Harriet were the perfect pigeons: a spinster lady (although Aunt Harriet had enough business acumen—she was after all Poppa's daughter—to suspect a pinch of chicanery) and a recently (and desperately) bereaved widow, two women raised not to question what men told them to do—another legacy of the diaspora culture. They did as they were bid, informed neither lawyer nor accountant, and sold the stock.

When he was finally told, their lawyer wanted to sue the principals for fraud and misrepresentation. "Why *didn't* you sue?" I asked my mother years later.

"Why make waves?" she said.

"Because the son of a bitch should have gone to prison." The son of a bitch in question was the harp sharpie Poppa had groomed at the bank, the one who had sweet-talked Do and Aunt Harriet, his benefactor's daughters, into the deal. I would occasionally see him at mass on Sunday, receiving communion, hands folded, tongue out to receive the host, a swindler and pillar of the church, and I would think, You pious fucking Yank-rimming hypocrite, I hope you rot in hell. I was perhaps also thinking about what my share of the stock would have been worth had Do and Aunt Harriet sought legal advice and not sold.

"What would that have proved?" Do said.

We got along, more or less, and more as the years advanced, as long as she did not have to comment on what I wrote, or thought. I dedicated my first book to Aunt Harriet, and when I was in Hartford shortly after publication, Do's friends would ask, when Aunt Harriet was out of the room, why I had not dedicated it to my mother instead. I would say I didn't have to, Do did not need that kind of certification. It was true, and yet I was careful to tell her the same thing, in case she too wondered. When I moved to California, I would call her every Saturday, and we would parse the week's events, in the world at large and in the world of the family. I was three thousand miles from Hartford and in those weekly calls she would un-burden herself as she might not have been willing to do had we been face to face, when she felt she had a side to uphold. (And over the telephone she could not tell me that my breath was bad.) The idea of family—the idea of a Catholic family—was important to her, even as all around allegiance to faith and family was growing slack. She had reached a kind of sepa-rate peace with a world she was willing to tolerate but did not appreciate, a world of the previously unthinkable in which the sons of her friends left the priesthood and one of her own sons got divorced.

I suspect I was a trial to her, the writer too interested in the possibilities provided by the sniper fire of family life, ambushes she chose to ignore, the happy family being as necessary an idea to her as the Catholic Church. Even about the Church we agreed to disagree; I was the fifth of six children, my father was dead, there was only so much energy she could expend to keep the family together, it was easier to pray for the repose of my soul than to force me to toe the line. Faith had never been my long suit, even in parochial school. Receiving the sacraments was a habit, like masturbation, and easier to break. My Catholicism was ad hoc; I called myself a Catholic, but I was no longer a communicant, nor did I feel bound by any strictures of the episcopate. Toward the hierarchy I held a cer-tain benevolent contempt; the Pope and his bishops had a cere-monial institutional value, like the Queen of England, but no applicability to real life. With an excess of enthusiasm, I would point out to her every abomination reported about the clergy. I remember especially the French cardinal who died in a prostitute's fifth-floor walk-up. Perhaps she was a relative, Do said. Or perhaps His Eminence was making a house call. Explanations I greeted with hoots of laughter, and wrote in my notebook. None of this raillery had anything to do with the being Do called God. I felt about God the same way I felt about the Kennedy assassination conspiracy theories: I was willing to believe but had not yet been sold. Then why call yourself a Catholic? she would ask over the telephone. Because it was a way to define myself, I would reply. Implicit in that answer was that being a Catholic was better than being a Yank.

Do died in December 1974, of cancer. From diagnosis to death was blessedly brief, four months. In the fall, my wife and I were lecturing at Yale and drove up to Hartford to spend some time with her. Through an exercise of will, she got herself out of bed, dressed, and made herself ambulatory for the four days we were there. We went for long drives and had lunch out, but mainly we just sat and talked, dotting every i, crossing every t. All her life she had been a tomb of secrets, but because she knew she was dying, she opened the tomb just enough of a crack to make me realize what an effort it must have been for her to maintain for so many years, in the face of all evidence to the contrary, the ideal of family, sanctified by faith and God's grace.

What would happen when marriages went wrong? I asked; we no longer had to maintain the charade that all marriages, even those of her generation, were made in heaven, and that if a marriage went bad, the only alternative was to "offer it up," as the priests in confession would advise. Drink, she said, and drugs. Drink, because wives did not work, live-in household help was plentiful and adultery was out of the question. Drugs, because they were available. My father was a surgeon and all his closer friends were doctors, this in an era when doctors, even surgeons, regularly made house calls, and carried narcotics in their medical bags, with morphine the painkiller and emergency drug of choice. I knew that my father had never carried morphine in his bag because several of his friends had become addicted; if a situation demanded a narcotic, he would call and order it from a pharmacy. Who? I said, wanting names, faces. Do would open her tomb of secrets no wider. Suddenly, thirty-five years after the fact, I remembered coded conversations around the dining room table, directed over the heads of the children. Dr. and Mrs. X, I said, pulling two names from the mists of memory. She did not deny it. How did you know that? she said. It was just a conversation I had been carrying around since the age of seven, and finally I had the cipher to crack it.

We left for California the next morning. I remember her waving goodbye in the driveway, no tears, knowing she would never see us again, my wife and I knowing our next trip to Hartford would be for her funeral. She went to bed immediately, never to get up. I would call her every other day, even as she grew steadily weaker. "There's one good thing you can say about dying," she whispered to me a week or so before the end. A nurse had to hold the telephone to her ear, and I could barely hear her voice. What's that? I said. "I won't have to read about Richard Nixon or Patty Hearst anymore."

The call to Hartford came the day after Thanksgiving. She was barely alive when we arrived, in a coma, but even with her shrunken body, a death rattle caught in her throat, this most fastidious of women was prepared for come what may, her hair fluffed and lightly rinsed, as if she had just come from the hairdresser, an expensive pink bed jacket buttoned around her neck. She died the next morning. I had hoped my last memory of her would have been the sight of her waving goodbye in the driveway, but instead it was of the funeral attendants removing her from the house in a gray body bag. I remember being surprised because I had always thought body bags were black. It was bitterly cold the day of her funeral, and I counted the number of women in the congregation who were wearing mink coats. I was already making notes for a novel. "The Right Reverend Monsignor Desmond Spellacy counted the mink," was the way I began a chapter in that novel a few years later.

III

STEERAGE TO SUBURBIA. Steerage was my grandfather, Dominick Francis Burns, D.F. to acquaintances, Dominick to friends, Poppa to his children—my mother and my Aunt Harriet— and to his six grandchildren. He came to Hartford from County Roscommon, from a town called Strokestown, and traveled from Ireland to the New World via Liverpool and New York, accompanied by his brother William, older by two years. When the Burns boys from Strokestown cleared immigration at Ellis Island, they boarded a riverboat and sailed up the Connecticut River to Hartford, where relatives from Ireland waited.

In family lore, the end of that journey from Strokestown to Hartford is encrusted with legend. My grandfather and his brother each had a card hanging from his neck identifying him as a Burns, according to Aunt Harriet. The time, we were all told, was the Civil War. There was further embroidery. Dominick Burns's first job in the New World was passing out casualty lists of Union dead and wounded, Aunt Harriet again the source, as well as Poppa's obituary in the *Catholic Transcript*, the weekly house organ of the Hartford diocese. "His stories of the Civil War days were many and vivid," the *Transcript*

34

wrote when he died. "As an immigrant boy, he went to the
Hartford station at train time in order to get the papers containing the latest news of the progress of the war." Because I
am a novelist, I extrapolated that the Burnses who were there
to greet my grandfather on his arrival were refugees from the
potato famine. Because I am also a journalist, I am forced to
conclude that the story about the Civil War casualty lists is
fable—the arithmetic does not hold up. Poppa was eight-three
when he died in 1940; Aunt Harriet said he was ten or twelve
when he stepped off that riverboat in Hartford. Born in 1857,
he then would have arrived no earlier than 1867, a lad who
had probably never heard of Appomattox or Antietam or Fred-
ericksburg or Second Manassas until he read about them in
his curiosity to find out about this strange place where he had
washed up. The novelist grieves that the journalist has a head
for numbers, but he is not so assimilated that he has forgotten
an Irish refrain from his youth: "And who's to say it isn't
true?"

In the hallway outside my office, I have six photographs of
Poppa in a single frame. The first was taken when he was a
young buck in his twenties; there are two in his thirties and
one each of the man of property, at forty, fifty and eighty. His
education—family lore again—ended in the fifth grade. From
1874 until he died, he was a grocer in Frog Hollow, a section
of Hartford that the poor Irish who lived there would have
been too proud to call a ghetto, its proper description. Frog
Hollow abutted Park Street and was a community of male
Irish laborers and female Irish domestics who worked farther
west in the households of rich Yanks. They lived in tenements, two- or three-family houses, with six to eight people in
the two bedrooms, kitchen, and parlor of a single apartment.
For the Irish in Frog Hollow, upward mobility was available

only via the three *p*'s—politics, the priesthood and the police department. "That was the only way a Mick got out of the Hollow," I have a character say in my novel *Dutch Shea, Jr.,* a character I called D. F. Campion, the D.F. initials for Dominick Francis, after Poppa. "The Yanks wanted to keep us there, and don't you forget it."

Poppa prospered as a purveyor. First he was a clerk in a meat market, his hours, according to a newspaper clip on the occasion of his eightieth birthday, from four in the morning until nine at night. Then, in 1881, he became a proprietor. In his store at the corner of Park and Lawrence streets, crackers came in barrels, molasses and vinegar in jugs, tea and coffee in boxes. There were no paper bags; everything had to be scooped, then wrapped in butcher paper twisted in cornucopia shapes. The fledgling grocer became a successful grocer, finally a rich grocer. He founded a bank—The Park Street Trust—a block from his store, moved out of Frog Hollow and became a man of substance in the city of Hartford, but until his last illness, when he was well over eighty, he still went to his grocery store every day, put on a straw boater and a white grocer's coat, this bank president emeritus, and waited on customers. I can recall him even now, reciting Irish poetry ("Ah, cruel was the fate that impelled me to part / From those scenes, now in exile, so dear to my heart . . ."), his pockets as ever full of change for his grandchildren, lifting first me and then my younger brother, Stephen, so that we could pick our own cookies from the cookie barrel.

Poppa returned to Ireland only once, in the summer of 1907, a fiftieth-birthday present, I would infer, to himself. He traveled alone, his wife and two daughters—Aunt Harriet and my mother—left behind in Hartford. (My grandmother was his second wife; his first wife had died childless.) That this was a solo venture without the companionship of his family was not altogether surprising. As if by rote, the women in Poppa's family deferred to him and the rules by which his conduct was ordained. He was temperance, although men were generally absolved from his strictures against strong drink, I suspect because my father, a not insubstantial presence himself, with a habit of command earned over a quarter of a century as a surgeon in an operating theater, would have told him, however politely, to go piss in his hat. Not so my mother. Even as a married woman in her forties, with six children of her own, she would never smoke or drink in front of him; if he came to call, ashtrays would be emptied and traces of lipstick removed from highball glasses. Poppa's attitude toward women was conditioned both by his culture and his religion. Women were meant to keep house and propagate the faith, no more; anything else was putting on airs. A clue to the way he might have felt about what the culture called the weaker sex, the fair sex, is found in a yellowing clip pasted into his scrapbook, cut from God knows what newspaper and called "About Women":

When a woman gets cross, she gets cross at everybody.

Smile at some women and they will tell you all the troubles they ever had.

When a woman can wash flannels so that they will not shrink, she knows enough to get married.

A woman is never so badly in love that she does not try to find out the cost of her engagement ring.

You occasionally find a woman who thinks she is intellectual because she has a large number of correspondents.

Poppa was the most careful of men, and I would also infer, giving him every benefit of the doubt, that perhaps he left his wife and daughters behind when he returned to Ireland because he wished to spare them any pain in case he was disappointed by the mother country he would encounter after an absence of thirty-eight years, if indeed he would discover that the reality of the place did not measure up to the memories with which he had regaled them and nourished himself. In his telling, he received what he called "a royal welcome. People came from all over the country to see me. They'd look at me and say, 'Billy Burns's son.' " The only account of that trip comes, again, from his obituary in the *Catholic Transcript*, not always, as I previously insinuated, the most reliable of sources, especially as it applied to any achievements, real or fancied, in the lives of the archdiocese's more eminent Catholic laymen. "When the ship that brought him back to Ireland was nearing shore," the *Transcript*'s story said,

> he stood on the deck alongside the late Supreme Court Justice Oliver Wendell Holmes. Justice Holmes had a pair of binoculars through which he was scanning the shore. He turned to Mr. Burns and said, "Well, Mr. Burns, you must be anxious to see your native land. Take my glasses." Mr. Burns thanked the Justice and, to repay his courtesy, recited a poem in praise of the Irish countryside, to the delight of Mr. Holmes and of other passengers nearby.

Irish gentleman meets quality, quality is impressed, a fairy tale of the immigrant experience. But who's to say it wasn't true?

IN A MONOGRAPH on immigrant Hartford, prepared by the Urban Studies class at Northwest Catholic High School, Poppa was called "the saint of Frog Hollow." Every Thanksgiving and every Christmas, he gave dressed turkeys to all the poor who lined up outside his store to receive them. Money, he firmly (and to my mind, madly) believed, was meant to be given away to the less fortunate. He despised government charity with the same fervor with which he practiced personal charity. "If wishes were horses," he liked to say, "beggars would ride." For his philanthropies, he was made a Knight of St. Gregory by Pope Pius XI, on the recommendation of the Most Reverend Maurice F. McAuliffe, bishop of Hartford. And when he died, prayers were offered for Dominick Francis Burns even in the Protestant churches, a mass said in the chapel of the Episcopalian Trinity College, whose campus was tangent to Frog Hollow. His passing was marked by editorials in the two Hartford newspapers, Yank mouthpieces both. "Democracy shows itself at its best in such men as Dominick Francis Burns," said one, and in the other he was hailed as "Grocer, banker, churchman, friend."

I wonder now if there was not another side to this grocer, banker, churchman, friend, which no one saw, or cared to investigate. When my Aunt Harriet, nearly ninety herself, finally went to a nursing home, she delivered into my safekeeping the scrapbooks he had kept throughout his life. The contents of the crumbling newspaper clips were nothing if not eclectic: "The Vanderbilt ladies are said to possess $500,000 worth of laces," said one. "The Astors value their stock of laces at $300,000." There were dozens of loony Irish proverbs: "To be red-headed is better than to be without a head." And: "Don't give cherries to pigs; don't give advice to a fool." And: "The priest's pig gets most of the porridge." Another clip contained an "Old Rhyme" called "Color of the Bridal Dress":

Married in white, you have chosen all right.
Married in red, you will wish yourself dead.
Married in green, ashamed to be seen.
Married in yellow, ashamed of your fellow.
Married in pink, your spirits will sink.

There were cures for baldness and instructions on how to sharpen a carving knife and further instructions on the use of potatoes as an aid to washing: "To wash clothes without fading them, wash and peel Irish potatoes; then grate them into cold water." One clip was a list of admonitions that appeared under the simple headline "DON'T":

DON'T neglect your hands, and above all, avoid carrying blackened fingernails.

DON'T speak ungrammatically. Study books of grammar and works of the best authors.

DON'T pronounce incorrectly. Listen carefully to the cultivated people.

DON'T say "awfully good" or "awfully nice"; "awful" was never intended for any such use.

Some of the clips hinted at a suppressed antagonism toward those cultivated people to whom the immigrant was supposed to listen carefully. "FACTS ABOUT IRELAND," read one headline, quoting a letter from the *Liverpool Daily Post*, September 24, 1889:

PERSECUTIONS OF ALL KINDS

CATHOLICS AND THEIR BUSINESSES OPPRESSED
CRUELTIES UNPARALLELED IN THE HISTORY OF THE WORLD

And then followed two columns of restrictions imposed by the English against their Catholic subjects in Ireland:

Catholics were deprived of the franchise.

Catholics were not permitted to possess a horse worth more than 5 pounds.

Catholics (except in the linen trade) could not have more than two apprentices.

Catholics were not allowed to buy land from a Protestant, to inherit it from one, or to receive it as a gift.

No Protestant woman worth more than 500 pounds might marry a Catholic without forfeiting her estate to nearest Protestant heir.

Catholic orphans to have Protestant guardians, and be brought up in the Protestant faith.

As if in counterpoint, there was another yellowing clip, "CATHOLICS IN AMERICAN HISTORY," refuting allegations, "in several denominational papers," about the minimal part Catholics were said to have played in the establishment of the republic. The first such Catholic was Christopher Columbus. And after Columbus:

John de la Cosa, a Catholic, was a famous companion of Columbus. He acted as his pilot.

Americus Vespucci, from whom America accidentally received her name, was a Catholic.

And Ponce de León and Vasco da Gama and Ferdinand Magellan and Cortez and de Soto—Catholics all. And Samuel de Champlain and Isaac Jogues. "The Ohio River was first discovered by De la Salle, a Catholic. . . . General James

Shields, who obtained the first charter for the city of Chicago, was a Catholic."

These were the anarchist papers of Dominick Francis Burns, the saint of Frog Hollow, Knight of St. Gregory, man of property, grocer, banker, churchman, friend.

*

IV

For the immigrant Hartford harp, the way was still west, as it was from Ireland, across Prospect Avenue, a social barricade as intimidating as the Atlantic. Prospect Avenue was the border between Hartford and West Hartford, the frontier beyond which lay assimilation and ultimately deracination. (I remember a saying from my youth about this economic excursion of the immigrant Irish: "The first generation makes it, the second generation enjoys it, the third generation loses it.") West Hartford, and, farther west, Farmington, was the DMZ where the Yanks lived, the Yanks who owned the black balls that controlled the membership rolls of the Bachelors' Club, the Cotillion Club, the Junior League and the Hartford Golf Club.

I grew up in West Hartford, the ne plus ultra of the immigrant Hartford Irish dream. My parents' house on Albany Avenue had a six-car garage, and looked out on the house of that quintessential Yank Thomas Norval Hepburn, a urologist and pioneer in social medicine, but best known as the father of Katharine Hepburn; our summer house in Saybrook was only a hop, skip and jump from the Hepburns' house in Fenwick. I must confess here a certain lack of enthusiasm for the public and cinematic persona of Katharine Hepburn—the feisty lady of quality, a tad feistier and with a tad more quality than anyone else within range. She has always seemed to me all cheekbones and opinions, and none of the opinions has ever struck me as terribly original or terribly interesting, dependent as they are on a rather parochial Hartford definition of quality, as reinterpreted by five decades' worth of Studio unit publicists. This obiter dictum is, I admit, not a majority view.

Ours was a world of Haviland china and private schools and a retinue of help (I am still not Yank enough to use the word "servants") in the three maids' rooms on the third floor. My homogenized generation was acutely aware of the uneasy social relations between our affluent parents and the even more affluent White Anglo-Saxon Protestants, acutely aware of the difference between grocery money and insurance money. At one very social wedding between a Catholic girl with the right credentials and the scion of a Yank family, it looked as if two separate receptions were being given, one for them and one for us. Only the younger generation crossed the no-man's-land between the two groups. At a posh Connecticut beach resort where practically all the cottages were owned by Hartford people, a snack bar and notions counter divided the line of beach cabanas into two equal sections. One section was entirely Irish, the other entirely Yank. The Irish called the two sections the House of Commons and the House of Lords.

Each winter the Irish would devour the newspaper accounts of the young men and women who were invited to join the Bachelors' Club and the Junior League or to come out in the Holly Ball, to see if any Irish Catholics had made the grade. My sister Virginia finally was accepted as a Junior League provisional shortly before her age would have eliminated her from consideration. "My God," she said to me, "I'm thirty years old and the rest of the girls are just kids. I must be the oldest provisional in history." Final acceptance into the Junior League depended on a series of tests to ascertain the social skills of each provisional. One of the tests was to write a report interpreting a famous painting. The painting given Virginia was Brueghel's *The Peasant Wedding*. I wrote the report for her, copying it from a book I found in a library, assuring her that the Yank provisionals did the same thing, that they knew no more about Brueghel than she.

There were also more subtle differences between us and the Yanks. Their maids were usually either colored (the ethnic description then in vogue) or old family retainers. Ours were always wayward young women from the House of the Good Shepherd, girls of Eastern or Southern European stock with sexual histories and hair under their arms; one of my brothers once stuck a wad of gum into the hairy armpit of a sleeping Portuguese named Linda, a teenager with enormous tits and, it was whispered, one illegitimate child and another on the way, the result of a liaison on her day off, the result of what we called "doing it." Where she "did it," where they all "did it," constantly fevered the imagination; I used to think the House of the Good Shepherd was put on the earth just so I could jerk off. Linda disappeared as they all did when a period was missed—and as my mother was the dispenser of Kotex, no missed period went unnoticed—back to the Good Shepherd nuns at what my brothers and sisters and I called the House of Bad Girls.

I became a cloned Yank, slightly ashamed of my origins, patronizing toward the Irish still on the make. I called Poppa a banker rather than a grocer and said my father had graduated from Harvard—a half-truth; he had graduated from Catholic University and Harvard Medical School. The right schools were important in hastening the process of assimilation—the right Catholic schools, because as it was acknowledged that we were going to sectarian colleges, we needed some Catholic preparation to avoid the censure of the clergy. A "right" school sent a large percentage of its graduates to the Ivy League schools; Canterbury and Portsmouth Priory were in, Cranwell and the Catholic military schools were out. Though she had sons who graduated from Harvard and Williams, my mother had always wanted a son to go to Yale, because Hartford was a Yale town; Yale was where the Yanks went.

My idea of rebellion was to go to Princeton rather than to Yale. At Princeton, I developed a jaded sophistication much valued at Hartford debutante parties. A Hartford debutante—there is the definition of an oxymoron. Imagine my mortification when, as a Princeton undergraduate holding up the bar at a New York nightclub, I was asked by a Harvard type where I was from. "Hartford," I said, with the nasal whine I had adopted to distinguish myself from those I had taken to calling the lower orders. Outnasaling me, Harvard replied, "I think I've heard of it."

This is what it had come to: I not only wanted to be assimilated, I was ashamed of being Irish. As if pursued, I tried to distance myself from those who found the middle to their taste. I would be no friend in court; I was a hanging judge. It took me nearly a quarter of a century to realize that here was the tension that gave me a subject.

BLESSEDLY the cultural transplant did not take place. The gutter Irish spleen rejected the faux Yank cells. Frog Hollow was always true north in my magnetic field. Seven years at a parochial school within its borders made me comfortable with its ethos, and I am still fluent in its dialect. Hartford, in shanty Frog Hollowese, is minus the *t*, and the *r*'s are swallowed— thus "Ha-f-d"; Wethersfield Avenue becomes "Withersfield Av." The people with whom I went to St. Joseph's Cathedral School defined their neighborhoods by the parishes where they attended mass. "Where you from?" Not to answer "Immaculate" (for Immaculate Conception) or "Our Lady of Sorrows" or "LaSallette" or "St. Lawrence O'Toole's" was to be revealed as a heathen at best, a Yank at worst. I remember the nuns who taught me at St. Joseph's School—Sister Marie de Nice, Sister Theodosius, Sister Barnabas—more clearly than I remember the members of the history department at Princeton.

In my youth, if not today, a parochial school education— Catholicism itself—was predicated on the idea of sin, first original sin, almost immediately absolved by the sacrament of baptism, and after that all the transgressions against the Ten Commandments, with their attendant punishment. The seven deadly sins did not figure; pride was what a mother felt when a son became a priest, a daughter a nun. Confession was Catholic psychoanalysis—and it was free; the relief to kneel and say, "Bless me, Father, for I have sinned. . . ." It was in the confessional that I learned how to lie, to seek the perfect evasion: "I had impure actions four times." An odious phrase, "impure actions," but it was out of the question to say, "I beat my meat four times." I have always felt, on the basis of no canonical evidence, that the Catholic devout were encouraged by the clerical police to believe in a hierarchy of sins, with the abuses of the flesh top-seeded. The Catholic view of sexual conduct is layered with ambivalence. If you are taught from kindergarten that the only function of sex is the propagation of the faith, then the idea that there might be pleasure in eroticism becomes a source of guilt. I had five siblings, and I went through prepubescence thinking my father had three times more fun than fathers with only two children (although what form the fun took I was not quite sure), and nowhere near as much as Beans Murrihy's old man, who had eleven and who, it was said in the lavatory, where we went to smoke and vigorously shake our bald members at the urinal (masturbation was still beyond our ken), did it all the time, eleven times, Jeez Louise, I'm going to have forty kids, forty fucking times you can do it!

It was at St. Joseph's that I first began to accept as a given the taint on the human condition. The Sisters of Mercy who ran St. Joseph's were like steelworkers. If they had been born men, they would have had tattoos of the Sacred Heart of Jesus on their biceps and worn T-shirts with a deck of smokes rolled up in the sleeve. Sister Robert was the ringleader. She had a red face and rimless glasses and an eighteen-inch ruler that she swung as if she were a Crusader and the kids in her homeroom a bunch of infidels. The line on Sister Robert was that she would hit you until you bled and then she would hit you for bleeding. If that didn't work, there was always Father Hannon, the principal, who was a mean man with a rubber hose. This led to a rather sullen bunch of malcontents in the schoolyard, where your status was based on the number of times Father Hannon had whacked you with his rubber hose. The champion in my group was Jakey Shea, who won the honors by lighting up a Camel one day in class. Jakey was in the fifth grade at the time. He was also trying to grow a mustache, a feat beyond the wildest ambitions of the other young Catholic men in Sister Robert's homeroom. Jakey was finally expelled in the seventh grade when he asked Sister John Bosco why it was you never read about nuns in the newspaper. Sister Robert would have smelled a rat and dropped him in his tracks, but Sister John Bosco had an IQ about room temperature. Naturally she said it was because nuns did God's work quietly. "Nah," Jakey Shea said. "It's because who the fuck cares."

That, I would have to say, is the true harp voice, the voice of a man with a chip on his shoulder the size of a California redwood. And it was in that atmosphere that I found a voice. Let me emphasize that a writer's voice does not have to be nice, and if the voice belongs to someone of Irish extraction, it rarely is. I think this comes from an inbred hatred of the Brits, and by extension a distaste for all Protestants. The parochial schoolyard is a breeding ground of class hatred; it was there that I became suspicious of all authority, of anyone who would speak for me. The Irish voice is one that essentially gets a kick out of frailty and misfortune; its comedy is the comedy of the small mind and the mean spirit. Nothing lifts the heart of the Irish caroler more than the small vice, the tiny lapse, the exposed vanity, the recherché taste.

Although it is not necessary for a writer to be a prick, neither does it hurt. A writer is an eternal outsider, his nose pressed against whatever window on the other side of which he sees his material. Resentment sharpens his eye, hostility hones his killer instinct. A writer *is* his voice, and his voice is determined by memory, and memory depends on who he is and where he comes from. It has to be mined, dug out, held up against the light. It does not extrude naturally from the subconscious onto the page. It is easy to look back now and say that what transpired followed from A to Zed. It did not. The resentment was under control. I was too busy trying to be a Yank during a lot of this time, from the Holly Ball to Princeton to the Stanford University School of Business.

I actually was accepted at Stanford Business School. "What do you want to be?" my mother had said as I approached graduation from Princeton. I cleared my throat and allowed languidly that I thought I might like to write (and that is exactly how I said it), as if the young debs at the Holly Ball constituted the audience I was after; "to write" implied a trade, and moneygrubbing, while "I thought I might like to write" implied the gentleman amateur, who would write in much the same manner as he played squash, just another leisure activity. The reaction from my mother and Aunt Harriet was as if I had said I had gone soft for an altar boy. "How do you expect to make a living doing *that*?" Aunt Harriet said, "that" spat out as if it were the sin that dared not speak its name. Business school was the alternative Do offered, and I applied to keep her off my back; Do was one of the many to see I had no negotiable skills, and maybe two years at business school would shape me up, get me over "this stage" (writing as a career was always seen as "this stage"), make me less likely to make waves. Do was always trying to shape me up. When I was sixteen, she sent me to one of those academic concentration camps so favored by the Irish and the Catholic. My misdemeanor was stealing a gross of condoms while working at a summer job for a wholesale pharmacy. Not that I had any voraciously agreeable partner in mind. I was still a virgin, and would remain one for a few years more, but within my breast beat the heart of a romantic.

A romantic now signed over to the Stanford Business School. I so hated this idea that I volunteered for the army. Consider me as a draftee—a middle-class Irish Catholic with a stutter, a degree from Princeton (a very undistinguished degree from Princeton, I might add), the politics of an alderman, and social graces polished to a high gloss at the Hartford Golf Club. What I wanted most in life was to be an Episcopalian. What I became was a PFC in a gun battery in Germany.

V

THE DUKE OF WELLINGTON always maintained rather cheerfully that his armies, the armies that brought Napoleon to ground, were composed of the "scum of the earth, the mere scum of the earth." The Great Duke was just warming up: "The English soldiers are fellows who have all enlisted for drink—that is the plain fact—they have all enlisted for drink." And again: "Some of our men enlist from having got bastard children . . . you can hardly conceive such a set brought together." Two years as an enlisted man taught me that nothing had really changed since Waterloo. There were judges in shit-kicker jurisdictions, patriotic men of probity, who offered men with whom I served a choice—the county farm or Fort Chaffee, Arkansas. Forget the downy-cheeked lads and perky-knockered lassies, Wonder Bread white and *café au lait* black, who hype military enlistment in the TV commercials, waxing moony about the GI Bill and learning a trade, usually electronics: the other ranks and private soldiers of every army, except perhaps those informed by some revolutionary ideal, are still scraped from the bottom of society's barrel. Therein lies the subversive brilliance of *From Here to Eternity*. James

Jones clearly understood that an army is predicated on class hatred; patriotism is only a convenient piety ("all stuff, no such thing," Wellington said). I think it is because of my army service that I so detest *She Wore a Yellow Ribbon* and *Fort Apache* and all those cavalry classics John Ford made with John Wayne. Ford was a reserve admiral in the navy and he had an officer's romantic view of the military dynamic, a homoerotic bonding of the commander and the commanded, with Ward Bond and Victor McLaglen as lovable career sergeants who exist, there against the dawn and dusk vistas of Monument Valley, but to do for Lieutenant or Captain or Colonel Wayne. This is not art, it is the agitprop the haves use to keep the have-nots in line; Ford's bogus (and professional) mick sentimentality only lent color to an essential social lie.

From the day I was inducted as a recruit Private E-1 to the day of my discharge as a Specialist 4th Class 731 days later, I was a fuckup in a social order in which the fuckup was king. In basic training at Fort Chaffee, I lost my rifle—the military equivalent of a mortal sin, one without hope of absolution— and failed to qualify on the firing range with either the M-1 or the carbine. Because I was an assistant company clerk during basic—a parlay of my Princeton degree with the opportunistic taking of a typing course the summer before I was drafted—I was able to jigger my range scores to the lowest marksmanship qualifying level; the first sergeant covered for the loss of my rifle because I was his toady, gofer and supplier of beer, and would have volunteered to be his pimp if asked. He knew it and I knew it; here was the social equation of the basic training company, of the army itself, an equation that gave shading to the concept of fear and favor.

At the end of basic training, my graduate education continued in Germany, where I was assigned as a personnel clerk to a field artillery battalion. The *kaserne*, or post, had been a Luftwaffe base during the thousand-year Reich, and was perched on a hill overlooking a town called Wertheim, on the Main River fifty miles southeast of Frankfurt. Baker Battery could have carried its colors under Wellington. The battery commander was a drunk, the first sergeant had syphilis, and the medic was what we used to call in those days a homo. I shared a room in the barracks with the medic and his twink, a cannoneer in the gun section who did not have all his face cards. In the room next door there were a couple of brothers from Tennessee. Their last name was Jethro. Neither had a first name; the older brother was W. X. Jethro, the younger Y. Z. Jethro. Y. Z. Jethro once threatened to kill me during a barracks discussion of evolution; he claimed I said his grandmother was a monkey. Violence was avoided only by the intercession of Corman, the supply clerk. Corman came from a Bible-whacker college in the Midwest, and was the final arbiter on all matters of evolutionary theology. Corman and I became friends. It turned out that the Bible-whacker college had left not a mark on him. Back home, he had been fucking his mother's best friend, who would send him Kodachrome photographs of herself naked in what he called her rec room, an obese woman of middle years with heavy, pendulous breasts, one hand lost between her legs and the other holding the clicker for the camera, on her face what passed for a seductive welcoming smile. Corman shared the slides of every new photo session with me.

Down the hall in the detail section—an artillery battery was divided into the gun section, which actually manned and fired the 155mm howitzers, and the detail section, which handled communications, transport and the mapping of fire missions—lived a black PFC named Homer Reed. Homer had a mouthful of teeth like tombstones and a tongue that seemed the size of a glacier; when he laughed, which was often, the tongue rolled over and the middle of it extruded from his mouth, a mass of pink that appeared to have the consistency of tundra. Homer was the battalion card shark. In others words, he cheated. There was no card game he could not fix. Everyone on the post knew he cheated, and yet they still played penny-ante games with him, trying to catch him. On paydays, when the stakes were more serious, Homer would travel up and down the Main River to various army *kasernes* where his reputation did not follow, fleecing the suckers.

One day Homer asked me to be his shill. I had won his approval by doctoring his service record to eliminate some bad time he had earned for a stay in the base hospital with a dose of the clap (bad time was added on to the end of an enlistment). The proposition was simple: Homer would fix it so that I would win his crooked card games, I would keep twenty-five percent of the winnings and he the other seventy-five percent, with expenses off the top. I was thrilled to be considered—the offer was like a scholarship to the University of Hard Knocks—but I also knew that Homer's reasons were not entirely altruistic. His payday winnings were making his pigeons restive; they might think the college boy new to the game was too white bread to cheat. I finally turned the offer down, less out of any sense of moral outrage than for practical reasons. I was a terrible cardplayer. I was also afraid of getting caught and ending up a floater in the Main.

None of this was mentioned in my letters home during this period, which my mother saved and I read after she died. The

55

letters were insufferable, full of the fake gentility and noxious superiority of the entitled; I made the army seem like a disagreeable duty weekend with distant and poorer cousins who did not have my advantages. They were also, to a fault, self-consciously ironic, and "written," as if I fancied myself a budding Pepys (although one with no grasp of the language):

> I should begin by not making apologies for not writing these past four weeks, but apologies are both time consuming and space consuming & I have an abundance of neither. Suffice it to say that the dearth of my letters was not entirely due to my negligence. When I returned from Italy [I had been on leave], I returned to a carousel of administrative activity. Like a carousel, this bureaucratic furore seemed to go round and round without a pattern & without an end. The stimulant to all this purposelessness was the military operation known as "Gyroscope," about which I have written you and which indirectly concerns you as it will bring me home to the States in April instead of August. When there was a lull in the proceedings, I sought to wade through the obligatory Christmas correspondence—"wade" is a preposterous verb to use; one would think I had received a freight car full of presents. This is all in the nature of the apology which I had vowed not to make, and it all sounds like the rankest rationalization, but for the most part it is true. When I don't write, it is not because I do not think of you or because I am completely lazy; rather it is due to a subtle combination of circumstance and laziness, with circumstance the predominant ingredient in the mixture.

I could have been a Yank. And the circumstance that I did not deign to spell out was that I was spending most of my spare time fucking my brains out.

. .

WHERE AN ARMY is, whores are. Another fact of military history, and one that the army implicitly acknowledged by making free condoms available in the first sergeant's office, purchased out of the battery's petty cash fund. At Saturday inspections, the rubbers were lined up in the footlocker alongside the toilet articles—shaving cream, toothpaste, razors and condoms—in my battery the lineup by package size. Weekends I would go to Frankfurt to get laid. I had a car, a two-seater Opel I had bought for three hundred dollars advanced me by my mother, and after inspection I would change into civilian clothes, get my pass, show the CQ my box of rubbers and point the Opel toward the autobahn.

The whores in Frankfurt, as they did in most German cities, congregated in the *gasthausen* near the *hauptbahnhof*, or the railroad station. The *gasthaus* I favored was down an alley off the Kaiserstrasse. Even in the early Saturday afternoon it was jammed with GIs in civilian clothes, and stank of beer and sweat. I prided myself that I did not look like a soldier—my civilian uniform was a dark gray worsted Brooks Brothers suit, white button-down shirt, striped tie, and brown military-issue low quarters—but who except a GI or a whore would frequent that kind of joint. There were no black GIs in this particular place; the blacks had bars and whores of their own. I did not want to get laid that early in the afternoon; I just wanted to make sure the girls would still be there when I returned after dinner, that the MPs had not declared the *gasthaus* off limits since my previous pass.

I do not remember what I did during those afternoons before I returned to the Kaiserstrasse. I never had been much on sightseeing, so that I cannot really believe that I visited Goethehaus or the Historisches Museum or the Leonhard Kirche. I ate dinner early and by eight o'clock was back in the bar at the end of the alley. The point was to get an all-nighter; an all-nighter usually began at one or two in the morning, when the girl finished turning any other tricks that might be available, but if you arranged for an all-nighter you had to stay around the *gasthaus* without getting drunk. On a PFC's pay, the prices were not all that onerous, and except for the money my mother lent me for the car, I lived from payday to payday, ninety-odd dollars a month, which meant I could afford a whore every couple of weeks.

The whores were the sort of camp follower reserved for other rankers since the dawn of military history, the type referred to, in opera stage directions, as "women of the town." They spoke a kind of camp follower's English. "ZI, GI" meant "Fuck off" or "Get lost," ZI meaning, in military speech, zone of the interior, or the continental United States. Only rarely did they give public vent to their situation. "God, I hate to fuck you cocksuckers," I heard a girl say one Saturday to the GI with whom she was negotiating. She was the sort of whore who promised trouble, the kind I tried to avoid at all costs.

There was no romance. Hi, you free? How long? All night. You kidding me or something, GI, it's only eight o'clock. How long then? You buy me a beer then, OK, GI? The deal would be struck and then the two of us would be in a Mercedes taxicab—all the cabdrivers in Frankfurt drove Mercedes cabs, and I always wondered how they afforded them, the mercantile outlook of the Hartford Yank still in operation. We rode in silence, she occasionally giving the driver instructions in German, I wondering if perhaps he was her accomplice and I a mark for him to roll. Then we would arrive. It was time to get down to business.

This was the part I never got used to. Not the service, but the venue. Invariably the whore rented a room in an apartment in a working-class district, an apartment in which a family lived and went about its business as if the tenant were not practicing her trade in the spare room. I was thrown by the situation the first time. The whore unlocked the door and when I entered the apartment, there sitting around the radio was the perfect German nuclear family—husband, wife, aged female relative, preadolescent child. I thought it was the girl's own family. I nodded, perfect Yank Cotillion Club manners, and said, Hi, how are you, that nasal honk I still thought reflected quality and had not yet banished. A brief nod from the head of the family, who went back to his newspaper. The girl grabbed my hand and without even a nod to the family led me to her room—her bedroom, her home, her place of business.

It was not so much a room as an alcove, separated from the tiny parlor by a glass partition covered with thin gauze curtains. It did not have the sense of privacy I thought the situation required; I still did not know her relation to the family outside. There was a tiny bed, a few belongings in the cupboard, some family pictures, and a pair of rosary beads on the bedside table. I gave her the money and she took a sheet from the cupboard and spread it over the bed. We took off our clothes and lay on top of the sheet. The nuclear family was just a thin wall away. I wondered what they thought of the noises they must have heard coming from the alcove. It was inhibiting, but then the moment took over.

The whore was the first woman I had ever fucked who did

not shave her armpits—another cultural adventure. Between couplings I asked about the family on the other side of the glass door. It was with some relief that I learned it was not hers, that she was just renting a spare room. A combination of bedroom and sweatshop, I thought. We performed again, and then I got dressed. The whore told me to wait outside while she finished dressing. I wondered how I would deal with the family in the parlor. I sat on a hard wooden chair and tried to make conversation. Nice weather we're having. Mild for this time of year. You're really glued to that radio, it must be some show. Except that English was not spoken here. It was as if I were invisible; the family pretended I was not there. The whore came out of the bathroom that served the entire apartment, wiping between her legs with a towel as she vanished behind the glass door into her room. To the family she was as invisible as I was. Finally she was dressed. Neither she nor the family acknowledged each other when we left the apartment. Outside I hailed a cab, which took us back to the Kaiserstrasse. It was not yet ten o'clock, and I had no place to sleep unless I picked up another whore for an all-nighter. This was a transaction beyond my budget. I retrieved my car and drove back to Wertheim.

SIDELINE Q & A

I once attended a PEN lecture, one of those fund-raising events at which the rich get a chance to meet writers and get off on doing something for literature and the writers get a chance to eat quiche and drink Dom Perignon in a thirty-four-room apartment afterward. That evening's lecturer was a novelist, who said that between books he always began writing

his autobiography, and that when he began to lie he knew he
had started his next novel.

Q: How much of what I have written to this point is true?

A: Enough.

Q: What next?

A: The life.

PART TWO

VI

*TO My Comrades in the Resistance
concerning Cheka Occupation
Via Mexico. Cheka has learned
of our existence.*

THE ABOVE WARNING, if warning it indeed was, was buried under "Personals" in the classified ad section of the *Los Angeles Times* one morning in September 1979. I rarely read the classifieds and do not know what impelled me to do so that Wednesday morning. The other ads were standard stuff, either ambulance chasing ("If saw accident 1am September 1, Olympic/Crenshaw, call Mr. Rose 213/461-4961") or attempts to get laid ("Miss Jean Harbison, Class of '62, Newport Hrbr HS, would like to hear from you. Call Mike, 714-842-2050 days"). I looked at the ad for a long time, at the eccentric punctuation and the poetic configuration of the copy. Cheka. Lenin's secret police, forerunner of the GPU and the NKVD and the KGB. Was there an old Menshevik somewhere in the 213 area code, still afraid that Kremlin thugs were on his case? It was sixty-two years after the Russian Revolution, he would

65

certainly be nearing ninety, and probably not worth a hit except in the fevered confines of his own senility. But then again. Even paranoiacs sometimes tell the truth, sometimes even have a reason for being paranoid. "Via Mexico." Did that imply a Trotsky connection? "Our existence." Define "our." Who and how many? "Resistance." What resistance? What "occupation"? The questions multiplied, and the possibilities.

The possibility that laid itself out to me was this: A writer sees the advertisement. He checks it out. He checks it out because he is bored, or his marriage is in trouble, his girlfriend is pregnant, his child has been killed; this is the sort of detail that can be worked out later. For story purposes there will be an old Menshevik, alive and not too well in Redondo Beach, and somehow, just vamping here, it all works itself around to the KGB and the Hollywood sign and the Evergreen Cemetery in East Los Angeles and the pregnant girlfriend, Miss Jean Harbison, as it turns out, who was the single eyewitness to that accident at 1 A.M. at the corner of Olympic and Crenshaw and who in fact was impregnated not by the burnt-out writer but by . . . George Smiley, for this is the country of John le Carré, and unfortunately not mine.

I was, of course, at liberty. A writer at liberty is a writer without anything to do, and with no real idea of what he is next going to do. This is the time he spends constantly, omnivorously trolling for material, even in the *Los Angeles Times* classified sections. I had not the slightest interest in what happened to the old Menshevik, nor indeed did I much care if he even existed. I had of course considered the idea that the ad was an elaborate practical joke concocted for the likes of me. And that Cheka was only the name of a house pet. What the ad offered was a story, but it was one I had no fix on, no coordinates on my psychic chart to triangulate my position.

Writers are always being approached by people who say, "I've got this terrific story to tell if only I had the time to tell it . . ." Or "The things I could tell you about Dewey, Ballantine . . ." Or "The things I could tell you about running a coup in Panama . . ." In a word, bullshit. There are no good stories. Only the singer really matters, seldom the song. What a writer brings to any story is an attitude, an attitude usually defined by the wound stripes of life, and I had no attitude toward the Cheka warning.

An attitude need not be particular. A century or more ago, an English critic named Walter Besant incurred the wrath of Henry James by stating unequivocally that "laws of fiction may be laid down and taught with as much precision and exactness as the laws of harmony, perspective and proportion." One of Besant's laws was that a writer must only write from "experience," and he offered an example: "A young lady brought up in a quiet country village should avoid descriptions of garrison life." This injunction was like catnip to James. In a published reply called simply "The Art of Fiction," James wrote that while it would be "difficult to dissent" from Besant's "laws of fiction," it would also be "difficult positively to assent to them," because they were "so beautiful and so vague." A wonderfully elegant Jacobite rap in the mouth. "The young lady in a village," James wrote, "has only to be a damsel upon whom nothing is lost to make it quite unfair . . . to declare that she will have nothing to say about the military."

James of course was less interested in the village damsel than he was in what constituted experience for even one so sheltered as she. "Experience is never limited, and it is never complete," he continued. "It is an immense sensibility, a kind of huge spiderweb of the finest silken threads suspended in the chamber of the consciousness, and catching every airborne particle in its tissue. It is the very atmosphere of the mind; and when the mind is imaginative . . . it converts the very pulses of the air into revelations." The person on whom nothing is lost, James goes on, is "blessed with the faculty which when you give it an inch takes an ell, and which for the artist is a much greater source of strength than any accident of residence or of place on the social scale. The power to guess the unseen from the seen, to trace the implication of things, to judge the whole piece by the pattern, the condition of feeling life in general so completely that you are well on your way to knowing any particular corner of it—this cluster of gifts may also be said to constitute experience. . . . If experience consists of impressions, it may be said that impressions *are* experience."

WRITERS COLLECT impressions the way a lepidopterist collects butterflies. When I am not actively working, I read the obituaries before I read the front page, trying to find something, anything I might use. In an obituary the spaces between the lines tell all. Occasionally I am rewarded. I found this memorial in the *Princeton Alumni Weekly*:

> Jason Smith died of a self-inflicted gunshot wound August 22, 1986, in Flint, Michigan. Jason had been depressed and experienced difficulty in finding and holding jobs in recent years. In mid-1985, he lost his job as a printing salesman for Hancock Press in Atlanta, Ga. He moved into his mother's house after he and his second wife divorced.
>
> Jason had not kept up actively with Princeton affairs after serving as president of the Princeton Club of Michigan in the 1960s.

To Jason's mother Inez, and his children Fiona, Steven and Chloe, the class extends its sincerest sympathies.

Jason Smith (I have of course changed his name and the places and dates and the names of his mother and children and his former employer) was a contemporary of mine at Princeton, a class ahead of me, someone of whom I was aware but did not really know. He was in a fancier eating club than I was. A low observation, but one I note to indicate an internal rhyming scheme in those spaces between the lines. It was not Jason Smith, however, who interested me here. He seems to have been one of those wretched people who not only could not prevail, he could not even endure. But his anonymous memorialist—all the memorials in the *Alumni Weekly* are unsigned—there is a character I could write. I know him. I know his infarcted sense of entitlement, his deep satisfaction with himself. Only someone so totally self-absorbed could write something so insensitive, so oblivious to the pain it might cause Jason Smith's mother and children. He was like all those Yanks I so detested in Hartford, someone on whom I had a fix.

I cut the memorial out of the *Alumni Weekly* and pasted it in my notebook. I keep notebooks when I am at liberty, something I never do when I am in the middle of a project. It is almost as if I am trying to prove that the time not working was not misspent. On the shelves in my office, there are a dozen three-ring binders, each about three hundred single-spaced pages long, the notes I have made and transcribed between books. They are not diaries. Twice I have started a diary, and each time I abandoned it within a week. Keeping a diary the way that Harold Nicolson did, with its seemingly effortless congruence of great events and vanity fair, simply takes up too much time. Nor do I find an account of the social ramble all that interesting. It makes one's life seem only a chronicle of lunching or dining out, and hence an occasion of ridicule if published, when in fact its subtext is usually available only to the diarist himself. I once gave a cocktail party attended by two Nobel laureates, one a scientist, the other a poet. "Cocktail party for B&J," my daybook said. "Derek Walcott, Edna O'Brien, Harrison Ford, etc." What I remember about the party, however, is a couple, lovers a long time before, when they were both reporters in Vietnam. They had not seen each other since Tet. They sat on a Victorian couch with black chintz upholstery, a gift from my mother when I got my first apartment in New York thirty years earlier, and they touched hands, both hands, just the fingers. They did not speak, and as I passed I could imagine them entangled on that couch, the scene of so many of my own youthful sexual encounters. The couch is the key to that internal rhyme, not the movie star, not the Nobel laureates.

The point of a notebook is to jump-start the mind. "Fenton's—Toronto," reads one entry. A frigid night in March, a wind like a frozen stiletto off Lake Ontario. I was in Toronto to give a reading, and after the reading I had dinner in a restaurant called Fenton's. At the next table there was a party of six, three men, three women, in their late thirties and early forties, engaged in an endless, relentless conversation about sex. All talked about their "mates," women and men alike. "I am basically a monogamous person," one of the women said. "Hair the color of ginger, and I suspect ginger pubic hair as well," I had written in my notebook. "Stretch marks." The woman had a voice that carried, a self-absorption that was total. "My needs have grown with the years," she said. "I don't like to sleep alone. The kids understand." The other five at the table seemed to hang on her every word. Her ex-husband had brought "the kids," along with his new girlfriend, to see his parents. "The kids said they never mentioned my name. It was as if she were their mother, not me." A scene began to take shape, a scene I transcribed that night in my hotel room:

I woke up. She was in the kitchen making orange juice and cereal for the children. I found a bathrobe in the closet. It was tight in the armholes. Whoever it belonged to was smaller than me. "Ted," she said, "the kids were asking why I was making so much noise in the night."

"Really."

"I said I was having an orgasm."

I tried to smile at the children. The boy spread peanut butter on his toast. The girl said, "Are you a good lover, Ted?"

She could not have been more than ten. I considered the question.

"Mom says you're a good lover."

It did not seem my place to agree. The boy was licking peanut butter from the knife. "What's an orgasm, Ted?"

Discrete, and without context, not a particularly good scene. Just an attempt at jump-starting in which the motor did not catch.

THEN THERE IS the mail. Mail is an occupational hazard of the writer's life, with an upside and a downside. The downside is that scarcely a day passes without several sets of bound galleys being stuffed into the mailbox, along with the publisher's accompanying form letter (". . . an astonishing roman à clef . . . We would be most grateful if you would share with us any comments you might have . . ."); this of course does not mean that the publisher would be all that grateful if the comments shared were negative. Equally noxious are the requests. Universities rarely mention an honorarium when they invite you to lecture or to attend their annual writers' conference, or if they do, they imply that while their budgets are small, your participation in the world of literature will be more than adequate recompense for what is usually—given travel time to and from, and three days in situ—a week out of your life. "For your participation," read one recent entreaty, "we can offer travel to Tucson, conference registration, which will include tickets to planned meal events, and double-occupancy accommodations at the Westward Look Resort." For the uninitiated, "double-occupancy accommodations" means a roommate. Such requests, however, do perform an unintended service. They force the writer to contemplate, for better or worse, the realities of his financial situation: his overhead, his nut, the inequities of running what is essentially a mom-and-pop operation under a tax code geared to yuppie stock traders, now happily under indictment, and how it happens that an hour's speaking engagement in Tucson will end up costing him, travel and expenses and the shared room at the Westward Look notwithstanding, three weeks' work.

Wackos are the upside. "You still have not taken my advice and dumped that miserable piece of Jewish dreck you are married to," one letter says. My wife is a WASP from Sacramento. "I know, I know, you are going to tell me she is a WASP from Sacramento. B.S. She went to New York City anxious to break into publishing and came upon the idea that if she put on the Jewish Whining Act she could get published. Well, she succeeded all too well. Now her whole thing is permeated with the Jewish whine."

This correspondent is a regular. I only hear from him—I

don't think he is a she—after I publish a piece. His letters are postmarked from San Francisco, the return address each time to someone with a different Jewish surname—Goldman once, Appel another time—on a different street in Mill Valley; the letters always end with: "Name and address are fake." He seems to have studied the public record of my life rather more closely than I might have wished, or else—somewhat colder to the bone—is someone known to me. He is aware, for example, that my wife's family is in the real estate business, a fact that, while hardly a secret, is not all that available. He likes neither Jews nor my wife. He describes my lawyer as "a Hebrew" and Norman Lear as "just another Jew"; the reference to Norman Lear would seem gratuitous, except that Norman Lear is a friend and was, when I lived in Los Angeles, a neighbor, another piece of information not generally available. The regular's first letter concluded, "You don't think I'm going to sign this, do you?" It never crossed my mind.

Gerald (not his name) is another of this subspecies. He is an American airman stationed in the north of England. His letter was written in pencil on lined notebook paper, always a cause for some apprehension. Gerald had seen a photograph of my wife in a magazine. What moved Gerald to write was the way the photograph had displayed "the striking presences of your hand." The hand seemed just like a hand to me, but not to Gerald. "You see," he wrote, "I have an unusual interest in appendages. Particularly the larger ones. As has been my experience, large hands usually mean large feet as well." Gerald conceded that his interest in the larger "appendages"—a marvelously evocative word, suggesting that the appendages might be detachable—could be construed as "suspicious." Perish the thought. Gerald said he was "mindful of the world in which we live." Gerald cautioned my wife that "discretion is at all times Best." Gerald was himself so discreet that he gave as a return address a post office box number and not his unit designation—I would guess to counter any possibility that my wife would be indiscreet enough to forward his letter to his commanding officer. "I do hope you will consider the possibilities," Gerald wrote. "Why? Who knows?" Gerald then tried to answer his own question. "There exist in our life many routes, limitless paths, all leading somewhere. And it is to the open-minded and adventuresome that all things are possible."

The limitless paths Gerald might take I would advise avoiding; what Gerald might consider open-minded and adventuresome along the appendage line I prefer not to contemplate. And yet, while it gave pause to think of an appendage fetishist on the cutting edge of American nuclear strategy, I was quite taken by him. Wackos are important to a writer, because most of us have a professional interest in aberrant behavior, and the wacko who vents his rage or exposes his fetish opens a window onto the "real" world. Convict correspondents serve the same purpose. I particularly remember Eddie and the return address on the first letter he ever sent me: "SPSM. State Prison of Southern Michigan. World's Largest Walled Prison. Better Known as the Walled-Off Astoria."

I was hooked, as I was of course meant to be. Eddie had been a career sailor in the navy. He had written because he had read a piece I had done on a port where he once served on a navy tanker during the Korean War. This first letter was full of horror stories at sea. "That was the night we rammed our escort ship and killed most of the sailors of the Republic of South Korea," Eddie wrote. "So we lowered our lifeboats to go to the aid of the ship we rammed. Well, over the side for old Eddie. Did you ever try to pick up a body that's been

steamed to the raw bone? It comes off in your hands when
you try to lift it onto the stretcher."

Eddie sent me copies of *The Spectator*, "The World's
Largest Prison Weekly—7,500 Copies Circulated Weekly," as
its banner put it. "Lot of crap in it," Eddie wrote, "but the
prison white-collars eat it up. Looks good on the reports, and
a guy can make a special out of here on it." I read *The Spectator* avidly. One feature was "The Quarter Century Club,"
profiles of convicts who had spent twenty-five or more continuous years in stir: "After 33½ years behind prison bars,
JoJo today is a slow-walking, stoop-shouldered individual who
has felt the weight of these many years of disillusionment, dis-
appointments, discouragement, and most of all, distrust for
others." There were social notes: "Prison is a most unusual
place for a family to get together," began one, "but, down
through the years, SPSM has had its share of relatives doing
time together. Therefore, the brothers Bob and Billy Buick
are no oddity. The exceptional thing about the Buick brothers
is a sparkling personality that will attract most everyone they
encounter. Cap this with their excellent ability to get along
with people and you have their key to doing time."

The Spectator never mentioned why any inmate was doing
time in SPSM, just the length of his sentence, and the county
in which sentence had been pronounced. It was almost a year
before Eddie got around to telling me why he was inside. He
slipped it in, almost parenthetically, in the middle of what
amounted to his autobiography. He had left the navy, and his
wife had divorced him. "Well, by now I'm too old to go back
and finish my twenty years," he wrote. "Well, I run the country for a while and gets married again, that lasts about a hot
minute, and I'm in the joint because I off't her. But still, it's
not worth it, but what else could I have done, the way things

were." How things were remained unspecified, but apparently bad enough to impel him to off Mrs. Eddie. He then went on to tell me where I could send a Christmas package or a money order, was I so disposed. Our correspondence ended shortly thereafter.

VII

I AM ALWAYS jotting down first lines: "Billy Rutland was getting laid that night, which is how I happened to get the case." That is from a novel I might like to read, but know I will never write. My prevailing disposition tends more to the metaphorically gloomy: "The S.S. *American Dream* slipped out of San Pedro Harbor at midnight, with a cargo of death heads." And promptly ran aground before I could arrive at a second sentence. In my binders I also find endless lists of Irish names. The people in a novel are people the author is going to live with for two years or more. He is going to sleep with them, love them, hate them, betray and perhaps even murder them, and he must be comfortable with the names he gives them. Hercules Finnigan, Mouse McKenna, Wendell Gaffney, Sheila Mulvihill, Bones Brady, Dougie Doyle, D'arcy Degnan. None ever used, but I can tell by the alliteration and by the nicknames the kind of character I had in mind. A minor character. An assistant commissioner in the Department of Sanitation or the toastmaster at the annual communion breakfast held by the Knights of Columbus in St. Finbar's parish hall.

I find a short dissertation on names. "First the name. An

Irish name, of course. Not Sullivan or Meenan. Something more vague or less common. Which lets out the O's and the Mc's. O'Malley and O'Neill, McGuire and McDermott. Dunne is perfect, but out of the question for obvious reasons. Hackett. Not bad, but a touch bloodless. Fair, Flood and Clare. The same. Something more muscular but still ethnic. Mackey. Too heavy on the mick. Broderick. Getting warm." I finally used Broderick, but there was more than a hint of dissimulation in the entry. I was actually trying out a first chapter in the manner of Trollope—*The Way We Live Now* was the novel I had in mind—one I fortunately abandoned.

Newspapers and magazines are continuing suppliers, especially trade magazines and catalogs, the only publications to which I subscribe. *Soldier of Fortune* is a gold mine of gun lore, a bible of violence. In its pages, I note how to kill a man with a pistol, preferably an H&K P9S 45 cal. ACP, with a polygon barrel for increased accuracy. The objective is not to shoot the target in the head. That assumes that all parts of the head are equal. "The objective is a no-reflex kill." The objective therefore is to cut the medulla oblongata. The medulla oblongata is the widening of the spinal cord at the base of the brain. If one is aiming low, a shot into the motor nerves of the pelvic girdle will bring a target down. It is the particularity of the pelvic girdle and the medulla oblongata that I find of interest.

As well as anything Irish, anything Catholic. "Over the years, Father Cosgrove became known as the 'Dancing Priest' because of his dancing skills, which he used to deliver a spiritual message." That from a diocesan newspaper in Chicago—my reading is eclectic. A personal from the same diocesan paper: "38 year old mature male wishes to meet a Catholic female who has a strong faith in the Sacred Heart and the

Immaculate Heart of Mary. Not fanatical." Those last two words are the great touch. Sheila Mulvihill is a good candidate, devoted to the Sacred Heart, but not Nutsy Fagan about it, just the kind of Catholic female for Bart Hoolihan or John Murrihy, Vincent Cusick or Aloysius Kenna, mature Catholic males all. This clip comes from a wire service: A United flight makes an emergency landing in Denver because a casket in the cargo compartment has ruptured its seal, sending the noxious fumes of the corpse into the passenger cabin. I can see a pattern beginning to develop. Perhaps Walter Hackett was on that flight, and as a result of the unplanned stop in Denver, he met Sheila Mulvihill and ended up booking passage on the S.S. *American Dream,* having established before sailing that the best way to cut the medulla oblongata (all parts of the head not being equal) is by firing into the open mouth toward the center of the skull, the proof of the pudding being those death heads in the cargo hold.

OF COURSE not all the entries are so grisly; I just have a weakness for the grotesque, and its impact on the mundane. The ordinary is not without a code of its own. I invariably check the medicine cabinet if I use the bathroom in someone else's house; in a small apartment where there is no guest loo, entire medical, social and sexual histories can be constructed from the specific. Fiorinal means migraine, Flagyl a yeast infection, Naturetin bloat, Procardia and Persantine cardiac trouble. Valium, Librium, Enovid. The diaphragm, is it dusted or not? And in its plastic container? Is the extra roll of toilet paper on the back of the toilet or in a tasteful wicker box? Ty-D-Bol or Ozium for noxious odors? The towels, the fixtures: Czech & Speake is upmarket, a bidet piss elegant. Question: How many

American women actually use a bidet other than former airline stewardesses who become the third wives of rich Wall Streeters given to indulging them out of some quinquagenarian concept of passion?

In time, the habit becomes a tic, a kind of professional exercise, literary aerobics. Houseguesting one weekend in a rented summer cottage, I browsed through the owner's Yale yearbook and wrote down the names of his classmates who were in Skull and Bones. From the names I was able to make certain deductions. Bones is the most prestigious secret society at Yale, and twenty-four years after graduation no one of that year's Bones class had made so appreciable a mark on the world in either the public or private sector or in the arts that his name was readily recognizable. The owner of the house was not in Bones or any of the other secret societies, which suggested he was not what in his era at New Haven would have been called a big man on campus. He had also rented his house out for the month of July, which suggested that a summer rental eased the strain of the payments.

The house was located on the golf course of an exclusive club that only recently had admitted Jews; blacks wore white jackets and served. One of the members had married—a second or third wife—a black movie star, and there was conjecture at dinner about the possibility of scandal should he bring her to the club. In the late afternoon, as I watched the blond children of privilege and their equally blond au pairs bicycling down the narrow country lanes on their way home from the club, I was reminded of the comment of a friend of mine, from those years when I was living in California. "There are not only no blacks in Malibu," she said, "there are no brunettes." On this littoral there seemed to be no cellulite either, on au pair or maternal buns. I think this was why I was so delighted to find the foil of a condom, a Trojan-Enz, under my bed when I reached to get my slippers. Illicit ardor—illicit, or why the rubber?—amidst the artifacts of order and stability is like a feather tickling the erogenous zone of curiosity.

The long five-day weekend was slow and soporific—I don't play games and I don't much like baking in the sun—and so I warmed to the task of compiling a profile of the absent owner and his family, the family of *H. M. Pulham, Esq.*, as it were, the novel which, by chance, I had happened to bring along with me. The shelves were full of silver goblets and silver plates and silver tasting cups from the club next door. Golf, tennis, and backgammon. Win, place, and show. Father and son. Son and grandson. Mixed doubles. Second flight. Third flight. In the basement there was a family room adjacent to the swimming pool, and on the wall a montage of family pictures—children, father, and grandparents, cookouts in the sand, Thanksgiving at the seashore. Only one of the children's mother, at a *schloss* in Switzerland, alone with her husband. I wondered why no more. I knew the owner and his wife had not divorced; she in fact had given her tenants—my hosts—instructions about the maid. Of course. She was taking the pictures. Woman's work. It must have been she who took the photograph of her husband in Paris with a *clochard*. He was wearing a Burberry and a blue blazer and red golf slacks.

I wondered who she was. The towels in the guest bathroom were monogrammed "JPD." "D" was her married name. Then she was "JP" before she was married. A search of the bookcase. Another yearbook, from a Catholic women's college in New York, a school that Catholics thought tony, and WASPs only Catholic. There was only one "JP" in the class—short, dark-haired, extremely attractive, wearing a miniskirt, a younger version of the woman at the *schloss*. She was not mentioned

once in her senior class poll, which indicates she made no
more impact on her class than he did on his at Yale. She was
six years younger than her husband, and came from a smarter,
Park Avenue address—high ceilings and moldings and a
twenty-four-hour doorman—than his family's postwar building on the far East Side; he in fact had been born, according
to his yearbook, in Queens. Marrying up for him, marrying
sideways, at best, for her. His ushers, at their wedding sixteen
years earlier, had given them a coffee table from the Yale
Co-op, the kind that is usually banished to a country house
when the young marrieds can finally afford one, mock-brass
hinges and a mock-brass plaque, with the ushers' signatures
and the date of the wedding on it, screwed into the mock
mahogany. The table was in the library. There were leather-
bound books in the bookcases, but on examination they came
from a cut-rate book club that specialized in cheap leather
bindings for children's classics, *Black Beauty* and *Two Years
Before the Mast*. I bet my host that they lived at 860 Park
Avenue in town; when I checked the Manhattan telephone
directory, they lived fourteen blocks farther north.

I WOULD SAY I was keeping in trim, you would say you would
not want me as a houseguest, that what I was doing was the
equivalent of reading my host's mail; we would both be right.
The weekend, the cocktail party, the small dinner, the black-
tie benefit—this is work, the source of combat intelligence
from the social battlefield. What a writer must always remember, however, is that with rare exceptions—Edith Wharton
then, Louis Auchincloss now—he or she is never really *in*
society; a temporary visa is issued with the tacit stipulation
that it will be withdrawn and access denied if confidences are

betrayed. It was Truman Capote's mistake to believe himself a citizen of the world of fashion when in fact he only had a green card.

The smart writer expects to be deported; hands that feed are meant to be bitten. "She fucked her way to the middle": a female agent's evaluation of the stalled career of the female studio executive sitting at the far end of a dining room table in Bel Air. Another table, another day: "Women are to tennis pros what tips are to a waiter." And again: "Herpes are like Krugerrands. Everyone's got some." Even my wife is fair game. "I won't be condescended to by someone's second wife," she once told me bitterly. Into my notebook, except I made it a third wife, because everyone we know is on a second marriage. It was her material, she said. It belongs to whoever uses it first, I said. I steal scenes from old screenplays I wrote that were never produced; an unpublished novel I wrote when I was just a baby has been so cannibalized over the years that it is now just a pile of bleached bones. I was once chastised by another writer for using an incident, a stickup, that had happened to a third writer. My defense was that he should not have told it at dinner. The writer who took me to task would later use a robbery in which a mutual writer friend was the victim as a scene in a novel.

Admittedly this is scavenging; there is, however, no copyright on vanity fair. I remember a particularly odious evening redeemed only by an introduction to a woman who had been exposed to most of the famous and powerful men of several generations. She spoke in a peculiarly dated slang, as if she had been cloistered in a convent for most of the twenty-five years she had, in fact, been in public life. She said she was "having a ball"; she asked a waiter for "a weak Scotch highball"; she said a world-class swordsman was "a makeout artist."

In my notebook I wrote: "She grew up in a world in which not much was expected of women, and married into one in which everything was demanded, in which she was expected to move on an international scale, and she was found wanting." I rather liked her, but the cold-blooded professional bottom line was that her situation was too obvious. I did ultimately use her slang, putting it, appropriately enough, in the mouth of an ex-nun who had jumped over the wall after twenty years in the convent.

Sometimes I just noodle: "We had a post-coital discussion of the ablative case." And then again: "The mark of a truly sadistic school system is one that teaches *The Mill on the Floss*." True enough, but I wonder what provoked me to write it down other than my own inability to finish *The Mill on the Floss*, not to mention *Felix Holt, the Radical* or anything else by George Eliot. I think I just recognized a line with latent possibilities, a wild card. "This ain't the *Mayflower*, but your daughter sure came across in it." That one was easy, a shit-kicker's bumper sticker. "Prepare for *quenelles*." That was my wife, on our way to dinner at the home of a woman who serves spectacularly bad expensive food, the kind so labor intensive that only the very rich can afford the kitchen staff necessary to prepare it. "Sartre said revolution was seeing each other a lot." The fact is, I do not know if Sartre ever did say that, but the kind of character I had in mind would have intuited that not many others would know if Sartre said it either, and be smart enough not to say it in company where he thought someone might call him on it.

"Moral exhaustion is the AIDS of the criminal attorney." Something I jotted down in a courthouse. I haunt courthouses when I am not working. There is a drama in every courtroom—always a plus for someone who has difficulty with plot—and the language in the corridors has a demotic precision that calibrates class and resentment. "He's as smart as a box of rocks," a cop waiting to testify says about the city's district attorney, a man he called "Communion Breakfast McNulty," because the D.A. never missed one. Another courtroom, another view of the same D.A. "The Great Emancipator," a reporter says. "Not since Lincoln has anyone freed so many niggers." This is the way people actually talk, free of any specious public allegiance either to humanism or to racial harmony. Having a good ear simply means having a quick pencil, or a memory that does not leak. The lines are not necessarily to use; they are meant to fine tune, to perfect the pitch. "I like the cold weather," a dresser in a funeral home says. "The old people can't stand the cold and keel over in the snow. It's grand for business." And so was he.

VIII

THE NOTEBOOKS Graham Greene kept on two trips to Africa, one in 1941, the other in 1959, he subsequently published in one slim volume he called *In Search of a Character*; the character he finally found was Querry in *A Burnt-Out Case*. Writers travel, and they travel for the same reason Greene traveled, in search of a character. I make reservations in anticipation of a great adventure—there are wars out there and refugees and death squads and coups and colonels and the *intifada* and whores and charlatans and pansies—but as the departure date approaches and I look at the place names on my itinerary—Kuala Lumpur, Amman, San Salvador, Medellín, Monrovia, Jerusalem, Dubrovnik—a sense of dread takes over. I stock up on Lomotil and take a gamma globulin shot my doctor says I really do not need and wonder how I will get my laundry done and feel a sharp longing for the first world even before I receive my boarding pass for the third.

"Why am I here?" Graham Greene asked himself when he touched down in Coquilhatville in the Congo in 1959. It is the eternal question of the writer-traveler. Exit is what the writer thinks from the moment of his arrival. How do I get out? Is there a plane to . . . just some capital with a hot bath and a cold beer bottled by someone other than the local caudillo's second cousin from diverted USAID funds. And clean towels and water that does not need to be boiled or cured with Halazone. By the third day he has become a student, an exegete, of his own shit; constipation, a penance at home, is a blessing here, a divine anointing of the alimentary canal. Graham Greene again, a traveler over the world's troubled roads for more than sixty years: "In the eighth day I really feel I've had enough," he noted as he floated down the Congo, a Styx in the heart of the heart of darkness. "I'd like to be transported to a bathroom in the Ritz in Paris and then to a dry martini in the bar."

The plane to Paris unfortunately leaves only every other Thursday. The character, the place, remain to be found. Get the look first, and the weather. It does not matter what the city, what the continent; the central market is always ground zero: "Stall after stall of bananas and plantains and armadillo skins. Why armadillo skins? 'Por que armadillo skins?' My Spanish is no better than my French. 'Yo no se,' comes the answer. Three words which for me seem the national anthem of every Latin country. 'Yo no se.' " Rain and mildew, heat and dust; I tend to avoid places where it gets cold; as a traveler I prefer polo shirts and sunglasses and safari jackets and running shoes and combat boots and half-moons of sweat under the arms. "The pale moon and the pale stars . . ." This is Amman. "There is a period at twilight of similar magical light but more blued. A pink glow over all, a glaze, a sheen. A place where one comes to appreciate the minimal." Halfway around the world: "The Dutch colonial buildings in Jakarta are low, with red tile roofs and pale robin's egg blue shutters. The peculiar expressionist quality of the public sculpture. The West Irian throwing off of chains, the hands enormous, outsized, grotesque and troubling against the sky." I am not sure either description is even pertinent; one jots, and keeps jotting, in hopes that the figure will spring from the carpet. Back in the Western Hemisphere, on the way into San Salvador from Ilopango Airport:

> It was about a 45-minute drive in an embassy van with armor plate and bulletproof windows. A guard sat beside the driver with an automatic weapon in his lap [N.B.: ck make of weapon. Ingram Mac-10?]. By the side of the road children carried bundles of firewood and mangy red dogs roamed free. A herd of cows wandered unattended across the highway and the guard clicked off the safety of his weapon. For the first time one realized that this was a part of the world where someone might use a herd of cows as cover.

The stomach quiets and the eye starts to accustom itself to the local color. I am at an age where I no longer have much faith in the revelations to be divined in local color; the ironies are too insistent, too easily ascertained; in the eye of the beholder the colorful invariably patronizes the local. And yet I write it all down: the songs on the airport Muzak ("Raindrops Keep Fallin' on My Head" at Halim in Jakarta), the names of the stewards on Singapore Airlines Flight 112 (Wendell Ee and Morgan Ng), the signs on the houses between Bogor and Puncak ("Sweet Angel," "Cheerio," "Bunga Low"), the record store in the San Salvador shopping mall selling "Classics from Paraguay," the soldiers in the lobby of the Cine Morazan in San Francisco Gotera assembling a .50-

caliber machine gun in front of a movie poster of Jean-Paul Belmondo and Alain Delon in *Borsalino*. On Jordan TV, a woman anchor announces, in impeccable mid-Atlantic English, the presidential candidacy of Arizona Governor Bruce Rabbit. "Babbitt, rabbit," I write in my notebook, "we all sound alike."

Dinner in Jakarta. I am sitting next to the director general of the Indonesian Humor Institute. "Why so many dirty words in American films?" he asks, face abeam with good humor. "Shit, piss, son of a bitch." Same trip, same script, this scene at Gadjah Mada University in Jogjakarta. "The critical theories of Mr. I. A. Richards," asks the Indonesian lecturer, a specialist, he has said, in Fielding, Swift, Jane Austen and Conrad, "what think?" I was tempted to say, "Mr. Richards, he dead," but the temptation passed, and I said only that as I. A. Richards had died a few months earlier, I would leave it to history to evaluate his place in the critical pantheon, a rather elaborate construction for an Indonesian audience, for whom English, if they spoke it at all, was a fifth language, after Bahasa Indonesia, Javanese, Dutch and Japanese. It was also the construct of an imperialist, who did not have the foggiest idea about the critical theories of I. A. Richards, and was quite sure no one listening, with the possible exception of the lecturer, did either.

The aberrant eye begins to focus. "Good shrimp with peppers," I write in Kuala Lumpur. "At the next table, a Chinese keeps belting a bottle of Martell brandy. His party pays the check and departs, leaving him there, passed out cold on the table, his head in the rice. A cabdriver comes into the restaurant and drags him out, first by the shoulders, and when he can't manage that, by the feet. A corona of rice sticks to the drunk's face. Nobody moves to help, nobody appears to notice." And in Jakarta, a get-together with a group of Indonesian intellectuals:

> They were all Muslims except for Joan and me. I was the only one who drank, and I only drank the beer someone had bought for me at the embassy commissary. After dinner I talked about the therapeutic effect of holding a grudge. It was an attitude that shocked the Indonesians. Each assured me that no Indonesian ever held a grudge. I said I thought it more beneficial to hold a grudge than to slaughter 300,000 people as had happened in the 1965 bloodbath against the Communists. There was an embarrassed silence. Then one of the Indonesians said, "Perhaps."

East and west, I wonder how the local intelligentsia feel about being trotted out to meet the visiting firemen from America. The conversations are generally impenetrable. "I in Los Angeles once," my host said in Jogjakarta. "You in Los Angeles once?" I replied, falling into a kind of makeshift pidgin. I was eating pineapple upside-down cake, the dessert I was given every time I had dinner with Indonesians; it seemed the local idea of an Occidental delicacy. "Where you in Los Angeles?" "Manhattan Beach in Los Angeles." "Really?" "You know Manhattan Beach?" "My cousin lives in Manhattan Beach." I felt like a tennis player trying to keep the rally going. "First cousin?" "Second cousin." "Ah, second cousin." Then wild whooping laughter. "Second cousin," he repeated.

Why am I here? Unless he is Flaubert in Egypt or Henry James in Italy, the writer-traveler is not so much interested in learning about the country he is visiting as he is in establishing an attitude a character might have toward it. For the American writer, an American character. Wherever I have traveled in the world, I have been fascinated by the American abroad, and his (in my experience less so than her) peculiar inability to adapt to his surroundings. The diplomat is a case in point. In Indonesia, even the most junior officer in the embassy would have, if he was married, seven servants—gardener, night guard, cook, houseman, maid, driver and nanny. It is a strangely bifurcated life, lived in segments: two years in a hardship post, then thirty-three months in language school, after that three years somewhere else; I met one foreign service officer in Malaysia who was fluent in Thai, Finnish, Tagalog and Rumanian. For all the years abroad, a certain insensitivity prevails. I remember having a drink one evening in Jakarta with the ambassador. The servants were in white livery and passed warm, freshly roasted peanuts. I asked for a Scotch on the rocks and received a Scotch and soda. "It's part of the exaggerated politeness of the Indonesians," the ambassador said with booming bonhomie as he ordered the servant to change my drink. "They would never ask you to repeat your order." The houseman busied himself at the drinks tray and pretended not to hear. "That would imply you were not speaking clearly and would be impolite." My wife also jotted down the scene in her notebook, and quicker than I, she used it in a novel before I could.

Many Americans abroad tend to become faux aristocrats, assuming an entitlement to which they were not heir. In Singapore, I was particularly attracted to a youngish professor who was teaching something called American Studies at a local university. He was the sort of academic hustler one finds throughout the Far East, someone denied tenure at the Bozeman campus of Montana State University, but in Singapore an eminence with a literary chat show on Radio Singapore and a house and servants and no Montana winters. "A terrible man," I wrote in my notebook, "Lucky Jim in a safari leisure suit. He did not know the name of the little daughter of the Chinese couple who worked for him, an enchanting child fourteen months old. She had nearly died, living in his house, from some gastrointestinal illness, but still he had to ask the servant her daughter's name in that fake fluty Brit voice he had affected." He told me the third world had produced only one great novelist, and when I asked who, he said Paul Theroux. I was puzzled by the choice. Paul Theroux is a French Canuck from Massachusetts who lives in England. Then I remembered that he had once trekked this same third world academic highway, at much the same speed, and his clone was clearly hoping lightning might strike twice.

Why I am here? Because I am stuck, because I am bored, because I am desperate. I am a missionary in search of a thread, a narrative. On the plane to El Salvador, I write:

Watch for: a sense of self-importance, a slight inflation, a theatrical response. A sense of being on the world's stage. Who, before they became clients of Washington, ever cared about what these people thought, ever questioned them about their lives, their ideals?

In El Salvador, "the story"—the guerrilla war—has no surprises; rhetoric and death copulating once again.

There were two new helipads by the side of the river. It turned out the helipads were built right on top of a mass military grave.

The art of embalming is very primitive. Most of the coffins have windows so that the deceased may be seen. Wax is used to patch up bullet holes, but the embalming art is so primitive that the face changes color in the heat, but not the wax. An eerie effect.

In such situations of peril, I am attracted more to the peripheral—the female dwarf in the parish office in San Francisco Gotera or the gay piano player at the luncheon buffet at the Camino Real. He wore black eyeliner, his hair was styled and fluffed and he motored through "The Girl from Ipanema" and the theme from *Chariots of Fire* as if the keys were on fire, melody with his right hand, chords with his left, then a segue into "My Way." I found ironies in the telephone book: "N.B. In the yellow pages, the number of gynecologists who specialize in infertility. This in a country with one of the highest birth rates in Latin America." One day I had lunch with a local painter I had met at an embassy party. His grandfather had been a mass murderer of another era. He had ruthlessly put down an earlier insurrection, and was a madman, one who, in one of his regular radio broadcasts, had announced that it was "a greater crime to kill an ant than a man, because a man who dies is reincarnated while an ant dies forever." Hector, the painter, was a homosexual.

He is 42 [I wrote]. He is gay. His boy friend is seventeen, a cane cutter from Chalatenango Province. Hector has set himself up as a dealer in primitive art. This is how he gets boys. Most of the primitive painters are in fact boys. He encourages them to paint. The promising ones he lets work in his house. Because he has connections with the government, his boys don't have to worry about being drafted. His mother also lives with him. She is about four and a half feet tall. A heavy mustache and moles on her breasts the size of nipples. Hector calls her "Mommy." I suspect Mommy is aware of Hector's proclivities. All through the afternoon she was peeking through the curtains at Hector and his new friend. Occasionally their pinkie fingers touched on the couch. One of the death squads is named after Hector's grandfather. It is pledged to clean out not only *subversivos* but drug addicts and homosexuals as well from El Salvador.

The point is not just to learn what we are supposed to learn, to think that knowing the gross national product and the incidence of gastrointestinal disorders and the initials of the rival revolutionary factions and the implications of the failure of the coffee crop is any real guide to understanding a place. It is always best not to heed too closely what their embassy says or what our spooks say; the spooks are only of interest for the kind of running shoes they wear and how their hair is styled and where they stash their girlfriends around town. Nothing an embassy spokesman can tell me is as important as what V. S. Naipaul, another veteran traveler, calls "the chain of accidental encounters," that chain by which the writer hopes to reach something approaching critical mass.

Accident can define a place. In San Salvador one day, my wife and I were meant to attend some official function laid on by the government to show democracy in action. First the cab-driver got lost on the way to Ilopango Airport. Then, at 60 mph, the hood flew off the car into the windscreen. Stranded on the highway, we hailed another cab. This driver got off at the wrong exit, and we ended up at the civilian instead of the military airport. The official plane had already left. The day, however, was not lost. At the airport we bought tickets on a small plane to San Miguel, where the government was gearing up an offensive against the guerrillas. Late that morning, at the Zona Militar in San Miguel, I saw a young soldier in fatigues and a baseball cap, his AR-16 slung upside down on his shoulder, pressed up against the perimeter fence of the base. It took a moment for me to realize that he was getting a blow job through the chain links from the whore on her knees on the far side of the fence. An inchoate scene began to take shape for the novel I had not yet really addressed. A priest from the United States, an election observer, sees the incident. He does not understand why the girl is kneeling in the grass, her face against the fence, why the soldier's arms are raised, his fingers clinging to the links. "Does one of the other observers tell him? How? Better yet, does Leah [a leading character in the novel I had in mind] tell him? Yes, a woman. The embarrassment the world-weary cleric feels at not glomming on to what was happening."

An image like this is to understand what Henry James meant about the nature of experience: ". . . the power to guess the unseen from the seen, to trace the implication of things, to judge the whole piece by the pattern." Nothing I saw in the Middle East, no rhetoric I heard or violence I saw, was as vivid to me as a single moment at the Beqa refugee camp a few miles outside Amman. The camp was like refugee camps the world over—eighty thousand people crammed into jerry-built mud-brick houses, ten or twelve people in two rooms with an outdoor privy (the mysteries of procreation in such conditions available to the young even before they can identify the urges), garbage running in the streets, a snotty adolescent in a Boston Celtics T-shirt (T-shirt logos in the third world are, of course, staples of local color). Then a classroom of tiny Palestinian children, six and under, blue smocks for the girls, blue jumpers for the boys. The teacher was herself a Palestinian, born and raised in this camp, twenty years of stepping over shit in the streets. She blew on a pitch pipe and the children rose and sang a song in English:

> *Where do we come from?*
> *We come from Palestine.*
> *Who took Palestine?*
> *The Jews took Palestine.*
> *Why did they take it?*
> *Because it was pretty.*

That night I was scheduled to participate in a film symposium held by the Jordan Cine Club. I was staying at the Marriott in Amman. The hotel was crowded with drivers and pit crews for the Jordan Rally, a road race between Amman and Aqaba, won three years running by King Hussein's son Abdullah, a result that left a definite impression that the fix was in. The symposium was meant to begin at eight with a screening of *True Confessions*, a picture my wife and I had written, but by ten not a soul had shown up in the cavernous main ballroom except for the occasional race crew who wandered in, pirated the bread sticks from a table, and left without a word. Finally, at ten-thirty, the invited cineastes began to filter through the door, lavishing excuses: the Cine Club was having its annual elections, the balloting was fierce, we lost track of the time. There was one further hitch: someone had forgotten to bring the screen on which the picture would be shown. More excuses while a screen was tracked down. It was 11:15 before the picture began.

I stayed long enough to see that the sound was out of sync and then slipped upstairs to my room to pack for the 6 A.M. flight we were taking to Geneva the next morning. I came back down in time to see the last reel. The sound track was still out of sync. When the houselights came up, it was nearly one in the morning. Waitresses began serving food to the guests, perhaps thirty in all, who were scattered so far apart around the room I thought they were anticipating a hand

96

grenade attack. My wife and I were escorted to a trestle table in front of the room where we sat with the president of the Cine Club, whose English was dicey, and a Palestinian actor who would translate any questions from the Arabic.

The first question was in English. "There is a line in the picture, 'Looks like a leprechaun, stinks like an Arab,'" the questioner said. "How can you deal in such offensive and degrading stereotypes?"

I froze. I had not seen the picture in five years, but I knew there was no such line in the screenplay. I tried to remember the book, which I had written and from which the script was adapted. I tried to choose my words carefully. "You see, the sound track was out of sync . . ."

"You said 'stink.' I heard it. 'Stink.' We all heard it. 'Stinks like an Arab.'"

A murmur of assent from audience.

"The line actually was, 'Looks like a leprechaun, *thinks* like an Arab," I said carefully. "Because of the sync problem . . ." Sync, stink, think—I knew I was not helping myself out.

"But what does 'thinks like an Arab' mean?"

"It means sharp. Fast. Shrewd. Cunning." Scratch "cunning," I thought to myself. "Smarter than anyone." And then I added, a positive racial stereotype, "Like an Arab."

The answer seemed to suffice. An endless question in Arabic. The translator whispered in my ear, his voice picked up on the microphones and carried to the room at large. "Did your screenplay anticipate . . ." The translator sought the perfect words. ". . . the stately pace of the picture." Another pause to get the precise phrasing. ". . . the operatic staging . . ."

From the back of the room, a voice, in English, boomed, "He means boring."

More questions. It was now almost two in the morning. I

thought we would be there until it was time to go to the airport. Finally the translator said one more question, and he would ask it. "Is it Zionist propaganda," he said, "that demands you put an old Jew in every picture?"

I thought of that nightmarish scene in Graham Greene's screenplay *The Third Man* in which Joseph Cotten spoke to a group of book lovers in Vienna who thought they were going to hear a lecture on James Joyce when he was only knowledgeable about Zane Grey. Oh, shit, I thought, how did I get into this? And then I heard myself answer, my voice a kind of high whine, "There's no old Jew in this picture."

"Not in this picture, perhaps, but in most American pictures. Do the Zionists demand it?"

I played for time. "Give me an example."

The translator was by now quite exercised. "I mean, in every American picture there's a shot of some old Jew." He seemed to italicize *some old Jew* for effect. "An actor comes off a bus, there's a tracking shot . . ." He was fluent in the grammar of film. ". . . and the camera lingers on some old Jew in the bus."

"Mmmmm, yes." I could see two diplomats from the American embassy watching me uneasily, wondering how I would answer. I wished they had access to the lights, so they could have turned them off.

"Don't the Zionists think anyone else has ever suffered?" the translator asked accusingly. "Don't they think there was ever anything else besides their Holocaust?"

Still three hours before the cab to the airport. I wanted dinner, a drink, and to get out of there. The Holocaust was not a subject I was prepared to argue at two in the morning with an audience of Palestinian film lovers. "I suppose . . ." I examined every word for its possible impact. ". . . it is because this . . . experience . . ." I did not identify the experience as the Holocaust. ". . . is more . . . available . . . to American audiences. . . ." My voice trailed off. My wife whispered, "If he says because of Zionist propaganda, you're dead."

He did not.

Maybe he was just too tired.

Three hours later, we were checking in at Alia. Our bags were opened and searched at two checkpoints and at both a metal detector was run up between my legs, to the crotch and around the testicles. A guard removed my wife's menstrual chart from her cosmetics bag, stared at it for a moment as if it were in code, then at her and then at me, and when he finally realized what it was, he did not seem to know what to do with it. He dropped it on the counter as if it were a piece of incriminating evidence and waited to see if she would pick it up. We were with a friend, a *Newsweek* correspondent, and we sat for a couple of hours in the first-class lounge drinking orange juice and eating stale pastry. There was a delegation of senior Jordanian military officers in the lounge, each wearing a green beret and a shooting sweater. They were seeing off a Pakistani general in a splendid pale beige uniform with side vents and a tight blue Roman collar. We talked about guns. The *Newsweek* correspondent said that gossip about weaponry would melt the most rigidly correct Arab official. He said the French had done a survey on Chadian wounded in the war between Libya and Chad and learned that the Russians had supplied the Libyans with new small arms with so much muzzle velocity that a near miss past the eye could detach a retina and a near miss past the right side could rupture the appendix.

Time passed. The *Newsweek* correspondent said that security at Alia could not compare with the airport security at Kuwait during the Arab summit. He said the metal detectors in Kuwait were pitched so high that the clips on his suspenders set them off. The wire stays in the bra of a Reuters reporter had also set the detectors off. She had to retire to a ladies' room and remove her bra before she was allowed to pass through the checkpoint.

I began to muse. What a way to meet cute. A high-security third world airport. The male traveler laughing at the stranger who was forced to remove her bra. Then the man's clips set the detector buzzing. Their eyes meet. Cut to a hotel bedroom. A breeze through the mosquito net . . .

It was time to go home.

MEDICAL TIME-OUT

UROLOGIST: When you stand at a urinal and void, does your stream hit the back of the urinal or do you hit your foot?

PATIENT: I save the minor humiliations to add verisimilitude to the fiction.

PART THREE

IX

THE 1980S HAD BEEN the familiar season of death. First
Stephen. Then a year later my sister Harriet, with cancer.
Once again the family convened in Hartford; my brother
Dick and my sister Virginia lived there, I came in from California, my brother Nick from New York, where he had moved
after his sojourn in Oregon; he and I had not been in contact
since Stephen's funeral, and the subsequent exchange through
the mails about my various inadequacies. He and Harriet had
been close when they were children, Hat and I when I was
just out of the army and alone in New York. She called me
Johnny, the only person who ever has, and I called her Hat.
We belonged to a theater club and would go to a show on
Broadway together once a month—this was when I thought
the theater was smart; with age came wisdom, and an antip-
athy toward the stage and its practitioners I have long since
stopped trying to hide—and we would have dinner every couple of weeks.

In a way, Hat was caught in a cultural Irish American time
warp, victim of the differing expectations my mother's generation held for sons and daughters. My mother, widowed in

1946, pushed her four sons to leave home, but daughters were meant to marry, the sooner the better, and the type of Ivy League education lavished on the sons was not to be wasted on the girls; it was Marymount for them, or more upmarket, the Convent of the Sacred Heart, but never, ever the Seven Sisters. In true Catholic fashion, the mind was a vessel of doubt, and the theology of doubt had no place in a mother-and-homemaker's mental library. Hat was engaged briefly after she graduated from Marymount, but when that did not work out she was consigned by my mother and Aunt Harriet to spinsterhood; at that time, in that culture, a broken engagement was a temblor on the Catholic Richter Scale ranking just under divorce and a public acknowledgment of a loss of faith (the private loss of faith could be dismissed as "going through a phase," something to be dealt with in confession).

Hat was twenty-two. She was not exactly discouraged from getting a permanent job, the kind of job available today, and even then (in the early 1950s), to a bright, extremely attractive young woman, passionate about music (she had been a gifted violinist, not of concert stature but good enough to be a soloist at a college concert in Town Hall in New York), but the unspoken thought encouraged by my mother and aunt was that a job so interesting that it might prove difficult to leave could only harm her prospects, and the only viable prospect conceivable to them was marriage. Harriet never played the violin again after her engagement broke up. I never knew why (confidences were never easily exchanged in my family), never knew where cause started and effect ended, but I would occasionally come upon her, with the radio or the stereo system playing a classical piece, fiddling an imaginary violin in accompaniment, with all the bow and finger movements. The first time or two she was embarrassed, but after that she would just continue until the movement ended, or she got tired. It was lovely to watch and, I realize now, infinitely sad.

After her engagement ended, she had a series of more or less temporary jobs, first as a bank teller in Hartford, then as a volunteer running a gift shop at a New York hospital, jobs easily abandoned when my mother and Aunt Harriet would decide to send her on an ocean cruise to some remote corner of the world. I could never understand the idea behind these trips to unspeakable places; Bali comes to mind. They were voyages of the geriatric; if they were meant to expose her to the marriage bazaar, the only marriageable men were widowers of seventy-five, and they were already targeted by the shipboard merry widows; Hat was not yet thirty. At one point my mother and Aunt Harriet proposed to change their wills so that in the event of their death, Hat would inherit not one-sixth of their worth (one-sixth for each of the six siblings was how the wills had been written) but one-half, to see her through what they seemed to think was the shame of being unmarried; it was as if to them the scarlet letter was S, for spinster.

Hat did marry. I gave her away. She was thirty-two. She had two children, a daughter and a son. Then a lump in her breast that she left unattended, and she a surgeon's daughter who had grown up listening to my father talk about cancer at the dinner table. I can still remember those monologues, I can remember him talking about the smell of cancer, how it stank, how the stink clung to his clothes like cigarette smoke, how he opened a patient up and then closed her right up ("opened" and "closed," surgeon's lingo), she was too far gone, "riddled," the renegade cells had spread, *metastasized*, that word I have hated since childhood. I have wondered often over the years if Hat's failure to see a doctor immediately might not have been the result of never really emerging, even as a wife and mother, from that cultural cocoon where my mother and Aunt Harriet flourished, where they could shelter her, the spinster they never got over thinking she was, married though she might be. In this Irish Catholic warp, it was woman's lot to be passive; to be assertive argued for an independence that the culture denied. She was not assertive. She metastasized. She died. She did not live to see her daughter marry, her grandson born. Standing in front of her house that bleak February day after the service, someone took a photograph of the four surviving siblings. Two gone in two years. "I wonder," my sister Virginia said, "which one of us will be next."

She was.

Next, that is, among the siblings.

Five years before Virginia died, however, our brother Nick's daughter Dominique was murdered. She was twenty-two.

"Most of my friends have never been to a funeral," my daughter Quintana said after Dominique was killed. "I've had a murder and a suicide in my family." Quintana was sixteen.

I told her that eventually things would even out. This is the kind of placebo parents give children to help explain tragedy.

I am not altogether sure that things do even out.

QUINTANA IS an only child, and Dominique became her surrogate sister. For several years, when she was just beginning as an actress, Dominique worked part-time for my wife and me, earning pocket money as our secretary. She shared secrets with us, and especially with Quintana, and when my wife and I went out of town, she would house-sit for us. We knew John Sweeney, the man who killed her in a jealous fury, because he sometimes stayed at our house when Dominique was alone there with Quintana. In late October 1982, John Sweeney wrapped his fingers around Dominique's neck and strangled her for three and one-half minutes, choking the life from her body. He was tried for murder and convicted of voluntary manslaughter; he was sentenced to six and a half years in prison. With time off for time served, and with good time— one day reduced from his sentence for every day served with no serious breach of penitentiary rules—he was released from the Californa state prison at Susanville in two and a half years.

I did not attend the trial. A murder trial is an ugly spectacle, and had my own daughter been the victim, I would like to think I still would not have attended the proceedings. I do not say that others might not find catharsis in a courtroom; I only say it is not the place where I would look for it. I have watched too many murder trials, known too many lawyers and too many judges and too many prosecutors, to have many illusions about the criminal-justice system. Any trial is a ritual complete with its own totems. Calumny is the language spoken, the lie accepted, the half-truth chiseled on stone. In the real world, most prosecutors crave to be in private practice, where they would defend the same people whose crimes they claim, as prosecutors, debase society, offering the same ex- tenuating circumstances that are the object of their prose- cutorial scorn. Before the first preliminary hearing, I could predict that the counsel for the accused would present the standard defense strategy in cases of this sort: the victim, un- able to speak for herself, would be put on trial, and presented, in effect, as a co-conspirator in her own murder. The prosecut- ing attorney was equally aware that this would be the defense tactic; if he had been defending, he would have made the same decision.

At a deep level, the case involved a number of extremely

volatile questions about the relationship between the sexes, about male and female roles, about the role a woman's work should play in her life, about whose work and whose wishes should take precedence in an ongoing relationship, about whether a woman was justified in thinking herself independent—in other words, that whole complex of issues raised by women's liberation. People—a jury—would react to these questions strongly, and often in ways they would consciously deny. It was to these unspoken feelings that a defense attorney of any competence would appeal.

The maximum offense to which John Sweeney might have been convicted was murder in the second degree, and in California a conviction for murder in the second degree does not carry the death penalty. If John Sweeney was not therefore a candidate for capital punishment, then the state would have me believe that other lives were more valuable than Dominique's. This is a construct I cannot accept. My feelings about capital punishment are complicated. I would have been quite willing myself to do bodily harm to John Sweeney (or perhaps, to be more honest and less bombastic, I think that in a moment of rage I might have been willing), and with a certain ambivalence to have the state of California put him to death in Seat B in the gas chamber at San Quentin. (Seat A is used only if there is a joint execution; Seat B is the chair of choice because it is closer to the stethoscope tube used by the attending physician outside the chamber to pronounce the condemned man dead.) When the state, however, and its servitors decide that one life is more valuable than another, and one murder more heinous than another, that there are degrees of murder, some murders not even called murders but manslaughter, then capital punishment becomes a matter of bureaucratic whim, an intolerable idea. I would like to believe, nonetheless, in a justice regnant. I have worked what Edith Wharton called the underside of the social tapestry for most of my professional life. I know that the laws of nature, however aberrant, rule in any penitentiary system. I would like to believe that John Sweeney was buggered in prison—he was young and soft, perfect material for the cellblock punk—and if so, that at least one of the cons who sodomized him—no: fucked him up the ass—had AIDS, and infected him with it. It is an ignoble thought. So be it. I wish him every ill. I hope he dies as miserable a death as he inflicted on my niece.

X

In the waning summer days of 1987, Anton Siodmak was killed in a water-skiing accident in Portugal, where he went every summer to play tennis. Anton played tennis for a living. He was not on the circuit, and he was not exactly a hustler, but his ability on the court made him welcome at the better weekend tennis parties and gave him permanent access to the more elaborate N/S courts in Beverly Hills and Bel Air and Holmby Hills and Trousdale and Malibu. He charmed the men and occasionally slept, especially when he was younger, with the wives of inattentive husbands. There were even husbands, it was said, who implicitly encouraged this attention, because their tastes had become more catholic as the attractions of home and family had begun to pale.

After his lob, a stroke perfected as he edged past sixty, and one that maddened younger, stronger, but less talented players, Anton's most negotiable asset was his smile. He supplemented his income from the court, and the occasional bonbon from those bored and grateful wives, as a greeter in one or two of the more fashionable restaurants frequented by Hollywood royalty. He could be found just inside the door, where he would plant a kiss on both cheeks, in the European style, and laugh and exchange gossip and rearrange his datebook for the following weekend, singles here, doubles there, and the private screening on Sunday night, Marty's rough cut with a wild music track because Bernie Herrmann's score isn't ready, drinks at seven, dinner seven-thirty, we'll run the picture at eight, Costa's coming by if his plane gets in on time, and Sydney and Claire, and next Sunday, you cocksucker, it won't be love, love, I'll take two games. . . .

I did not know Anton all that well—I once made a stab at tennis but was glad to give it up when I broke my elbow—but I would see him at the odd screening, and when I ate at the restaurant he would kiss me on both cheeks and call me "Zhannee" and say that the dailies on So-and-so's picture were so lousy that the crew had stopped wearing the T-shirts with the film's title printed on them, a totem that in local lore was the kiss of death for any picture in production, it was a real stiff. When I learned he had been killed, I felt genuinely sad. He was an essential figure in the local community, because he had the gift of making people feel better, making them feel it was all right occasionally to be frivolous.

His memorial service was held, fittingly, on a private tennis court in Beverly Hills, a vast complex complete with its own bleachers, at the foot of a mogul's estate, a court to which Anton had had a key and where he could give lessons or bring the pigeons who thought they could take a set from him. The court was covered with Astroturf to protect the playing surface, and instead of seats in rows for the mourners, there were restaurant tables with bright cloths, and a bar, and gay waiters from the various restaurants where he had kissed the favored on both cheeks and passed on the latest scandal. It would be a party, we were told, not a wake; Anton would have wanted it that way.

I met my wife at the service, coming directly from a doctor's appointment in Santa Monica, and as I sat there under the hot August sun, death was very much on my mind. I thought Anton had actually died under the best possible circumstances for him, a moment of terror as he realized the inevitable outcome of the accident, then an instant later the eternal dark. I did not like to think of him sick or paralyzed, his smile and his serve no longer negotiable. The eulogists, all tennis partners or opponents, thought differently. They praised Anton's independence, which they claimed to envy, his ability to march to his own beat, free of all the responsibilities that came under the heading of "Making a Living." What most of the mourners, or celebrants, because this after all was a party, considered the highest praise came from a producer who said that in twenty-five years of friendship, a quarter of a century of foot faults and let balls, Anton "never once offered me a script." This was a code they all understood, implying that most damning breach of the local etiquette, the favor demanded by a retainer, and the subtext was that Anton knew his place. It was a subtext they could not articulate and would have denied if it had been so presented. They did not seem to understand that Anton *was* dependent, dependent on them, dependent, as it were, on the kindness of strangers. Had he a lingering illness or useless limbs, his currency would have been devalued, and he would have become a burden on these same friends, many of whom even now, at his memorial, his final party, could not properly pronounce, let alone spell, his last name. He was forever separated from them by a social barrier for which the tennis net was an apt metaphor.

The service ended and the parking attendant brought my car. As we drove away, my wife said, "What did the doctor say?"

There had not been an appropriate moment to mention my visit to the doctor in Santa Monica. "He scared the shit out of me, babe."

"What did he say?"

"He said I was a candidate for a catastrophic cardiovascular event."

INTERNAL AFFAIRS INVESTIGATION

Q: True?

A: More or less.

Q: More? Or less?

A: A name changed. A certain dramatic restructuring.

Q: Time collapsed?

A: By about two hours. But all the same day. And I am not sure whether it was that doctor or another doctor who said I was a candidate for a catastrophic cardiovascular event. I was on my way to Europe. A doctor, maybe this one, maybe another one the next day, asked how long I planned to be gone. I said seven weeks, including a month in New York. He asked where I was going in Europe. I said Germany and Ireland. He said do you speak German. I said no. He said how many good hospitals do you think you can find in the wilds of western Ireland. I said I have a feeling you don't think I should go. He said I think you'd be mad. He said I'm not going to say you're going to have a heart attack. You could live to be eighty without having a heart attack. I wouldn't bet on it, but it's possible. You have a history. Your father died at fifty-two of heart disease, your uncle at fifty. At this point, I think I mentioned George Santayana, you know, those who forget history are condemned to repeat it, but I am not sure. In any event, I am sure he would not have known who Santayana was. He was about eight feet tall and blond and very pleased with himself, really thrilled. He had that look like he thought he could fuck every nurse in his office and then go out and run the Santa Monica 10K. What do you do? he said. That pro forma question I aways dread being asked by doctors and dentists. "I'm a writer." The next question is invariably the same: "What kind of writer?" A good writer, I always want to say, but never do. Books and screenplays, I mumble. And then: "Would I have read anything you've written?" Dutifully I listed my credits, anticipating the blank look on the Adonis's face. Someday a doctor is going to ask me what I have written, and I am going to demand that he tell me first about his better prostate checks, what it felt like with his finger up someone's asshole. So whether it was this guy, this cardiologist, or my own internist the next day who said I was a candidate et cetera, I am not sure. It just seemed to fit better here.

Q: That's what you mean by dramatic restructuring?

A: If I did it, yes.

Q: Anything else?

A: When I told my wife he scared the shit out of me, I started to cry.

Q: Anything else?

A: I thought I was going to run into John Sweeney at the service.

Q: Why?

A: He was out of prison, and working as a chef in some restaurant in L.A. He knew Anton Siodmak. All those restaurant people know each other. He had worked for a lot of the people who were doing the catering that day. I just thought he might show up. As a matter of fact, one of his former employers called and asked if I was going to the service. I had the sense he was sounding me out so he could let Sweeney know whether I was going or not.

Q: What would you have done?

A: Left. I wouldn't have caused a scene. I was still shaking from what that doctor said. Also it was Anton's day for tribute, and a scene would have laid a heavy trip on his wife. She said the most poignant thing at the service. You had him during the day and in the evening, she said. I had him at night. At night, alone, then I think Anton would really have been interesting. At night he wouldn't have had to smile.

Q: Why did you spend so much time on Anton Siodmak?

A: Because it's a hell of a good story, and I'm a storyteller. Because the memorial service did correspond to the day the doctor scared the shit out of me. Because I like to play one thing off against another. Because I think nothing in life is ever discrete, and I know that is the second time I have used that word. I've also used "entitlement" twice and I intend to use it once more later on. And finally because I suppose some son of a bitch will probably do the same thing to me the day of my memorial service, if I ever have one, and if anyone comes.

IT ALL STARTED the day I received, unsolicited, a letter from my insurance agent. I have had a life insurance policy for over twenty years. I really do not know why. I have always distrusted life insurance as bad luck, a red flag waved in the face of fate. I pay my premiums quarterly, and try to ignore the fact that there is only one way anyone is ever going to collect. I am not exactly afraid of dying, although there are moments when I dream of becoming the first to beat the rap. My attitude toward death is essentially that of John Gotti, the mob Godfather. When his minions, in the summer of 1988, whacked out a wise-guy stool pigeon who was ratting on other wise guys to a federal prosecutor named Diane Giacolone, Gotti's benediction was: "Well, everyone's got to go sometime." The sometime I have in mind is later rather than sooner. Which was why I opened this letter from my insurance agent—a gentleman I had never met—with a certain reticence.

To my surprise, the letter said that my insurer, "in light of the many changes in interest rates and product design" (I especially liked "product design" as a life insurance concept), proposed to increase the value of my policy by fifty percent, with no raise in the cost of my annual premium. I have never thought of the insurance industry as a consortium of altruists, and I knew there had to be some benefit to them in this new product design, but a fifty percent increase was not to be dismissed lightly. There was nothing I had to do. A paramedic would come to my house, take my blood pressure, ask a few questions, fill out a form, nothing to it.

And so it seemed. The paramedic, a young woman, did make an appointment, did take my blood pressure, did ask the requisite questions: was I taking any medication, had I the usual string of childhood illnesses (measles, chicken pox), were my bowel movements regular and stool color consistent (I would rather be asked about venereal symptoms, about whether I ever had the clap or worse, than about my bowels; my childhood stammer returns and I avoid looking at the questioner as I try to guess what's a great stool color in the earth tones), had I ever had diabetes? As a matter of fact, I had tested as a borderline diabetic several months earlier, but I had gone on a diet and stopped drinking and my glucose levels returned to an acceptable plateau. No problem, said the paramedic. She would pass the results of my examination—it hardly seemed that; just twenty minutes in my library—to the insurer, who would check with my internist.

A month or so later, a second paramedic, also a woman, came to the house to repeat the tests, the first signal that perhaps I did not quite fit within the parameters of the new product design after all. The problem was that earlier glucose test; the possibility, if it existed, of adult-onset diabetes could disqualify me from the program. Would I see my doctor for a complete physical? Of course. A month later I took the physical. You don't have diabetes, my internist said, but it's time for your annual physical anyway, so let's put you on the treadmill and do an exercise EKG, which had not been on the agenda. Twelve minutes on the treadmill, a heavy sweat. Breathing heavily, still hitched to the monitors, I sat on a gurney as my internist read the printout. "You have a glitch," he said after a moment. What kind of glitch? "An abnormality," he said. It was the first of the terrible words with which I would become so familiar. As he tried to explain the significance of the squiggly lines on the EKG printout, I kept nodding sagely, feigning understanding, even though they were no more intelligible to me than the seismological charts you see on television after an earthquake. Is it important? I asked, still trying to appear casual. He was already dialing a number on the examining-room telephone. "I want you to see a cardiologist today."

I did not get the insurance. But if it had not been for the change in the product design of my old policy, I would not have taken that EKG. I prefer not to speculate about what might have happened if I had not taken the EKG.

·   ·

RIGHT OFF I was exposed to the Armageddon rhetoric of cardiology. What I had, according to the examining cardiologist, was a "critical lesion" in my left anterior descending artery, "a hemodynamically significant lesion," according to my internist. "Lesion" is one of those words, like "biopsy," that one can learn to hate very quickly. Another doctor, with what I can only construe as high cardiological good humor, told me that in the trade the left anterior descending artery was called "the widowmaker." My wife's internist, a no-nonsense septuagenarian Italian woman, who did not go to medical school until she was nearly thirty and who has never wasted an opportunity to speak her mind since, was quite vocal on the subject of this rhetorical inflation. "It makes them feel important to talk like that," she said. "You ought to sue the bastards for scaring you to death." There was of course another reason for the apocalyptic jargon: the fear of a malpractice suit. "They have to tell you the downside, the risk factors," my brother Dick said. He is in the insurance business and he had gone through a spell of cardiac unrest himself. "They tell you so you won't sue them, and they should tell you in front of somebody else so they have a backup in case you claim you weren't told about the risk." I had already noticed that there was always a nurse puttering about the room whenever the risks were detailed.

And so from the start I had a number of amiable conversations with my various doctors about the possibility of my dying. It is a subject that tends to concentrate the mind wonderfully. Quickly I fell into the trade lingo, casually referring to the left anterior descending artery as the LAD; it was a way of distancing oneself from the diagnosis, as if I were not the patient under discussion but, because of my familiarity with the arterial chat, a member of the medical team that was going to do its goddamnedest to lengthen those odds: we can't afford to lose this one, he's too important to the nation. No, to the world. I was voluble in singing the praises of my doctors—"They're the best, everyone says so, there's a medical conference in Shanghai, these guys are over there telling those Chinamen how to do it"—even though I had no empirical evidence that they were any more worthy medically than the pecker checkers who milked me down when I had my army pre-induction physical. Their putative ability simply became an article of faith; it made me feel safe to believe it, and feeling safe was the priority of the moment. I even praised the prints on the walls of their office, as if the quality of the artwork purchased by some medical decorator sanctified their professional skills. There was a Jim Dine in one examining room— "I know Jim and Nancy," I assured a nurse in that room one day, as if to tell her that the Dines were on my case, too, and watching out for me, making the painter's equivalent of a novena; she seemed never to have heard of Jim Dine—and in another examining room a print of Dunster House at Harvard; better Harvard than Chico State, I told myself.

My guru about my doctors was a very rich friend—Forbes 400 rich—who had come through two open-heart operations and funded hospitals. "They're really very good," he said. "But tell me, how many smart people do you know who went to medical school?" There was the canker on the rose, even for someone like me, the son of a surgeon. At that moment, I could think of only three, Walker Percy, Michael Crichton and Jonathan Miller, and none of them practiced medicine anymore. The mood shifted. Gloom. What sort of pretentious asshole would have a Jim Dine print in an examining room? Later I thought of Oliver Sacks and Lewis Thomas, both doctors, both smart (in the sense my guru meant, people with whom one could have a conversation about the larger world beyond medicine), but the damage had been done: that casual aside was a lethal injection into an already fragile psyche.

BEING A WRITER, I knew this was good material, and from the day of Anton Siodmak's memorial service, I began taking voluminous notes on every medical appointment and on all the wild thoughts that ran through my head, storing them in a file I called "Cardiac" on my computer. When my doctors used a term I did not understand, I would ask them to explain in detail, a tactic that sometimes made them annoyed, especially when I carefully wrote the answer down on a yellow legal pad, as it seemed to suggest to them that I was already preparing a malpractice suit. After I got home, I would check out what they said against the Merck Manual and the various medical dictionaries we kept in the house. I likened the situation to the time when my house was robbed twice within a period of six months: I got two pieces out of those robberies, and earned far more from them than the burglars did.

What I felt, oddly enough, was a sense of guilt, mixed with shame and embarrassment. It was as if I had been caught cheating, or in a public lie. One or more of my coronary arteries seemed to be occluded; it was my fault; I had put them at risk, in harm's way, because of my own bad habits, my failure to pay attention to my genetic history. Life halted. My wife had to go to New York to deliver a lecture, and to Miami to appear on a television show. The doctors had advised against my flying. "Go with her," I was advised by a friend with a cardiac history of his own. "If you stay here alone, you'll start writing your will in your head."

In effect, I already had. I was not exactly afraid. There was just a sense of constant apprehension, a feeling that I was living on borrowed time, that death was a constant companion; I felt like a soldier in the trenches, waiting for the order to go over the top. Every muscle spasm, every shortness of breath after the slightest exertion, induced an anxiety symptom. I found myself thinking I wanted to live until I was sixty, which was more than a hop, skip and jump away. There is something about having a "6" as the first digit of your age in your obituary. It is as if you have lived a full life, that you did not miss the allotted threescore and ten by all that much. I began to make small bargains with myself: I just want to see how the Bork vote comes out; I just want to wear my new suit from Sill's, it's all paid for, and I haven't worn it; I just want to give that reading at the 92nd Street Y in October; I just want, I just want. I saw omens everywhere. By accident I erased Susan Sontag's name and address from my computer telephone directory; Susan wrote *Illness as Metaphor*; I was going to die. The next day, by some electronic miracle I did not understand, I was able to retrieve Susan's file: I was going to live. I did not answer my mail; I did not want a letter to arrive after, the specifically unspecified after. I was ever aware of mundane last times: this was the last time I would have dinner at Morton's, the last time I would have a lube job on the Volvo, the last time I would have kung pao shrimp, the last time I would go to Dodger Stadium, the last time I would see a perfect pair of tits. Ah, sex, the last time this, the last time that, the last fucking hard-on.

"Milk it," I wrote in the "Cardiac" directory, "but no excessive melodramatics." I wrote, and then erased, an item about the logistical procedures I wanted followed in the event the unmentionable happened—for example, who would tell my daughter at college in New York (Calvin Trillin was to be given that honor); it was as if my wife, whom I jauntily called "the little widow," could not manage on her own. The entry was cheap and demeaning because I meant it to be read after the fact and make everyone cry about my sense of foreboding. Good sense prevailed. "Alt F4, block. Delete Block? (Y/N) Yes." It was all part of the distancing, an existential interlude.

XI

In MEDICAL TERMS, I was asymptomatic, meaning that until the glitch appeared on my exercise EKG, I had no angina symptoms, which are the early warning signals for coronary artery disease. My cardiac profile, however, was not without smudges. I was overweight, my cholesterol was somewhat out of whack, and most important, I was following in the genetic footprints left by my father and his brother. What appeared to be the narrowing of the left anterior descending artery placed the whole apex of the heart in jeopardy. Without medical intervention, I had an eight percent chance of a major, as opposed to a massive, heart attack. The chances of surviving a major heart attack were good, I was told, if I reached a hospital within the hour; with a massive heart attack, your survivors could start saying the prayers for the dying immediately.

The recommendation of my doctors was for me first to have an angiogram, a procedure by which a dye is shot into the coronary arteries; the dye would allow doctors to calibrate the extent of the occlusion. If the angiogram showed that the lesion was as critical as indicated by the EKG, the next recommendation was for a balloon angioplasty, or the dilation of the occluded artery by a balloon inserted into the arterial system. The balloon is inflated at the point of the occlusion and clears away the plaque (the stuff that dentists are always complaining about) causing the blockage. The analogy is inexact, but the effect is like that of a Roto-Rooter. With balloon angioplasty, the success rate is approximately three in four, meaning that in seventy-five percent of the procedures, the affected artery remains dilated; if the artery collapses again, the procedure is repeated a few months later, and if it fails a second time, then the option is for open-heart surgery. The chances of death during the angiogram were minimal, one in ten thousand, the Adonis cardiologist said, but during the angioplasty about three percent. A ninety-seven percent survival rate seems pretty good, unless you are the one who could be in that three percent, when your perspective on a near sure thing changes. Both the angiogram and the angioplasty were elective procedures. I elected to go along with the recommendations of my doctors: the angiogram, to be followed a week or so later, if the lesion was as hemodynamically significant as the doctors thought, by the balloon angioplasty.

Immediately I began hearing from friends who brought news from the cardiac pipeline about successful angiograms and angioplasties and open-heart operations. (Christopher Lehmann-Haupt, the senior book reviewer at the *New York Times*, was the only one who knew of someone who had died during an angioplasty procedure, but fortunately he did not tell me until some months after my own.) My former agent had undergone balloon angioplasty. ("He's too terrible to die," my current agent said, and then as if he had committed a semantic sin, he added, "Not that you have to be a terrible person to come through this thing; you're not a terrible person at all.") And a movie star I knew, although I was told to keep it quiet because the actor did not wish it to affect the insurance examination he had to take before every new picture. A woman friend who is no stranger to illness gave me the best advice of all: Don't be passive, she said, be an active participant in your treatment, even if that means being a pushy pain in the ass. "It is your life, John Gregory; no one is going to watch out for it better than you. And you are not your father. When your father died, they did not have these techniques. Now they do. Forget genetic history."

The admitting nurse at St. John's Hospital in Santa Monica, where the angiogram was to be given, had that Miss Ratched nurse-knows-best manner. I have often thought that the admitting staff at any hospital is picked solely for its ability to enrage the patients they are signing in, that indeed the patient's rising gorge as he is treated like a child while the paperwork is completed is itself a sign of health. Nurse Ratched asked what I planned to do while I waited for the procedure. Read, I said. "You can watch your soaps," she said. I said I did not watch the soaps. "Everyone likes to watch their soaps," she insisted. I said I would bring a book. "There will be no one to watch out for your book when you go down to the cath lab," she said. I said I would give the book to my wife. "Your wife will have to leave the room while you're prepped." Then I would give her the book before she left. "Most people," Nurse Ratched said, articulating every syllable deliberately, "are happy watching their soaps." I was beginning to crack. "They are not my soaps. I do not like the soaps." Nurse Ratched smiled. "Then you will have a new experience." She seemed to sense the murder that was further occluding my heart, and turned to my wife. "Wives can be little nurses too," she said. "You can help feed him. They're so hard to feed in bed."

I did not bring a book. I did turn on the TV set. But not to watch the soaps. It was the day Bob Fosse died. On the local news shows, on the network newscasts, on PBS and on *Entertainment Tonight*, every time I switched channels, I saw clips of *All That Jazz*, every clip ending with Roy Scheider singing "Bye, Bye, Life," as the Fosse surrogate's life oozes away after open-heart surgery. Bye, bye, life. Just the omen I was looking for.

The angiogram indicated that the LAD was ninety percent occluded. "Ao valve area calc 1.6 cm2," my report read. "Ao peak-to-peak gradient 27mmHg; LVEF 55% w/mild diffuse hypokinesis; calcific Ao valve w/decr mobil; non-dom RCA normal; L main normal; mid-LAD 80–90% stenosis, 1 cm distal to large D1; dom circ, OM2 1–1.5 cm 90% stenosis at 0.5 cm from origin LV 133/2; Ao 99/66; PA 24/17; PAW 13,10; CO 7.9, CI 3.5." In translation, it meant I was a catastrophic event waiting to happen. The angioplasty was scheduled for the following Tuesday, five days later.

NEWSPAPER HEADLINE,
Los Angeles Times, 2 October 1987

6.0 QUAKE ROCKS L.A.
AT LEAST 3 DEAD, SCORES HURT
HUNDREDS EVACUATE DOWNTOWN BUILDINGS

FROM A LETTER TO A FRIEND, *4 October 1987:*

Thanks for your note. I suspect I am the first person to have an angioplasty on Tuesday and have it tested by an earthquake on Thursday. I was in the old building at St. John's, up on the fourth floor, and it shook, really rattled. It was about eight in the morning and I was talking to the floor nun about getting out when it began to shake. "Sister," I said, "I think this is a fucking earthquake." "I think you're right, Mr. Dunne," she said, and grabbed the bed. I was holding on and she was holding on, and we were really rocking, and I kept thinking this is an old building, I hope it's built to code, and for thirty or forty seconds we shook. Thirty seconds doesn't seem like a long time, but thirty seconds of being terrified is an eternity. I was in bed, I couldn't get out, I had an IV in my arm, and a weight on my leg because I was still bleeding from where they inserted the catheter in my groin, and the pressure from the weight was supposed to stop the bleeding. I couldn't move. And I had this whole Catholic thing—I had said "fuck" in front of a nun. Anyway, I guess the angioplasty worked. When I apologized to the nun, I fell back into those evasions of the confessional. "Sister," I said, "I think I said a bad word in front of you."

It—the procedure, not the earthquake—was interesting in a scary kind of way. Casual conversation about a catastrophic event tends to point the mind in the direction of codicils to the will and the order of the speakers at the service, the moral decision being whether I have too much residual Catholicism to go the nondenominational route, with "The Battle Hymn of the Republic" rather than Gounod's "Ave Maria."

This is how they do it. They make an incision in the left groin and from there they insinuate a catheter up the arterial system into the coronary arteries. There is a live monitor on which they can watch what they are doing and another monitor attached to a VCR that tapes what they just did. They snake that baby up a few centimeters, then they play back what they just did and plot the next move. It's like they are reading a Michelin map of the ticker. When they finally get to the blockage, they inflate the balloon at the end of the catheter, the LAD is dilated, and if everything works the way it's supposed to work, the plaque is dissipated, and floats out through the bloodstream like shit through a goose. Then we hope that the artery stays dilated.

On the day of the procedure, I am barbered in the groin, giving me at my advanced age my first Mohawk, like those pussy Mohawks women have to get now so they can wear the new bathing suits that are cut so narrowly. Then a 10-mg Valium, backed up by a Valium IV. The procedure demands that the patient be sedated but not comatose, as he must respond to commands and answer questions. I say to the doctor, "I don't think I've been this stoned since 1968." "Few of us have, Mr. Dunne," he says, "few of us have." There was even background music, via a high-tech stereo system in the cath lab. It was playing a rather dirge-like Bach chorale when I was wheeled in. Then my doctor complained that he hated choral music and demanded some Mozart, so Mozart it was.

There was also a surgical team on standby, in case I have a heart attack during the procedure. The surgeon had, the day before, given me the surgical risk factors, throwing in one I had not considered, AIDS from a contaminated sample of the whole blood reserved for transfusion. In my Valium haze, I start thinking about this blood and I began babbling to the doctor that the man who checked into the hospital just ahead of me was one James "Jimmy" Dunn, and I did not want to get his blood type in case of a catastrophic event. The admitting nurse had made that mistake initially—I got his name tag and he got mine, and he had a different blood type. I think the doctor thought I was going bonkers about Jimmy Dunn, but I wasn't. He was wearing one of those charcoal gray utility outfits that drivers of soft-drink trucks wear, with "Jimmy" stitched in yellow thread over the left breast pocket. The doctor kept nodding gravely. "My son goes to Brown," he said from somewhere west of left field. "He takes a lot of English courses. He wants to be a writer, too." The "too" was the decidedly antic touch.

Anyway, it's over. I watched the whole damn thing on the monitors, an out-of-mind-and-body experience immensely abetted by the Valium, like a mescaline hallucination. There was a movie years ago called *Fantastic Voyage*, about a journey some miniaturized people took up someone's bloodstream, and that was what this was like, except I was the set, and God the production designer. With doctors and nurses and the procedures and the CCU and nurses and a private room, the gig is going to cost about forty grand, which is the only reason I continue to write movie scripts that don't get made, because the Guild insurance will pay for the whole nine yards. I would like to get some of this into the screenplay Joan and I are currently writing, but the script is supposed to be about Bugsy Siegel, and I don't think angioplasty would have saved Bugsy's bacon, his demise being the definition of a catastrophic event.

TEN DAYS after the angioplasty, I took an exercise echo cardiogram. The results, my cardiologist said, were "spectacular." A month later, another exercise echo, and again the results were "spectacular." The six-month test was equally good: the LAD had remained dilated, I had lost twenty-five pounds, my cholesterol was way down. "You've bought yourself a new life," my internist said.

I did not tell him the question it raised: What the fuck do I do with it?

The first thing I did was move.

INTERNAL AFFAIRS INVESTIGATION (*cont'd*)

Q: Isn't that a writer's transition? "In the summer of my nervous breakdown, I went to live in Las Vegas, Clark County, Nevada." You've used that trick before.

A: All writing is essentially a series of stylistic tricks. That kind of transition is just one of them.

Q: Was the move as much cause and effect as the transition makes it appear?

A: No. The move was not really because of the cardiac procedure, although it was a contributing factor. I was terribly depressed afterward, the way you are depressed after finishing a book. When you are working on a book, your entire life is focused on it for a period of time, then it's over, and the only thing to do is start again. It's depressing to think about, especially as you get older. You know exactly how long it takes, and if you live out your biblical life-span, you know exactly how many books you have left in you. Writers never retire, so knowing how many books you still might write is not exactly a reassuring thought. I remember years ago going up to Wellfleet to visit Edmund Wilson. It was Thanksgiving weekend, a couple of years before he died. He was in his mid-seventies, but he was still on the come, he still needed money the way all writers need it. He said sometimes when he couldn't sleep he would get up in the middle of the night and read old reviews of his earlier books. There he was, perhaps the one great man of letters this country has produced in this century, and he still needed that reassurance, even when it came from his inferiors. It's a tough way to make a buck.

Q: So the depression was like the postpartum depression of finishing a book?

A: More or less. For five weeks, my life had been concentrated, perhaps melodramatically, on whether I was going to live or die. Then it was over. It turned out OK. But it was a fucking anticlimax.

Q: Why do you say "perhaps melodramatically"?

A: Because of Vince Dooley.

Q: The football coach at the University of Georgia?

A: Yes. He had an angioplasty just about the same time I did. He leaves practice one day, goes into the hospital, has the procedure, and the next Saturday, there he is on the sidelines, yelling and screaming and coaching his football team as it beat up on somebody. He didn't seem to make that big a deal out of it.

Q: Maybe that's why he's a coach. It does not seem to be a profession in which introspection would be much in demand.

XII

I HAD LIVED in Los Angeles for twenty-four years, nearly one-eighth the history of that republic for which we stand, one nation, indivisible, with liberty and justice for all. I was at mid-life, that word it is fashionable to follow today with the additional word "crisis." Twenty-four years, nearly a quarter of a century, five houses, seven books published, four film scripts produced, a million or two words pounded out on type-writer and computer; a marriage that survived, a daughter born and raised to her majority, three siblings dead, plus a mother and an aunt, a suicide in the family and a murder; more acquaintances than friends, my fault, dead friends, lost friends, abandoned friends, friends that simply melted away; a few enemies, perhaps more than that, I don't really know, because I am generally indifferent to those who would be hostile; some triumphs, many small treasons, a quarter of a century not without incident, happy families are all alike, each unhappy family is unhappy in its own fashion. There was no crisis. The cardiac unrest only accelerated a process already begun. We had stayed too long at the fair. I felt tapped out, our life needed a goose. It was time to move on.

We put our house on the market. We would insist on our price, our leavetaking would be long and languid, perhaps we would change our mind, our departure—up violins—would make too many people too sad. The house sold the first day. There was now no turning back, unles we wished to pay the six percent commission to the real estate agent as the penalty for our indecision. There were a few recriminations. My cousin, a newspaper columnist in San Francisco, was reproachful. I hope, he said, you are not going to move back east and then tell the world how terrible California is, a perfect place, as Fred Allen once said, if you are an orange. I replied that I had liked Los Angeles well enough to spend most of my adult life there by choice, an answer that left him unimpressed, his cool silence making me feel, as I think it was meant to, a bit like Benedict Arnold.

We would live in New York, from where we had come twenty-four years before. Our business was there—in the sense that our business was defined by agents, lawyer and publishers—as well as many, perhaps most, of our friends. Nearly a quarter of a century in Los Angeles, moreover, had given us a remarkably clear view of New York and its epic pretensions, pretensions we found endearing. New York is at once cosmopolitan and parochial, a compendium of sentimental certainties. It is in fact the most sentimental of the world's great cities—in its self-congratulation a kind of San Francisco of the East. The place has a tabloid mentality; the gossip columnist is its Pepys. Lepke Buchalter surrendered to Walter Winchell, Suzy gets invited to lunch with Raisa Gorbachev. There is the romance of the Mob and the romance of the prosecutor. There is the romance of the press and the romance of danger—New Yorkers can't get over the fact that Houston and Detroit, cities out there somewhere, have higher murder rates. One has the sense, sometimes, that New York wants a recount, or its murderers to work harder.

We already owned a small apartment in the city, a pied-à-terre we had bought four years earlier, but it was clearly not big enough as a full-time residence where two writers might live and work. We needed a larger place. Advice was immediately forthcoming. One of the things that has always struck me about New York is the number of people willing to instruct me, with an almost punitive intensity, on how I must lead my own life. These instructions are always offered in the same spirit as those given to a callow recruit rifleman new to a veteran infantry platoon. Follow these instructions and you might have a chance to survive; if you do not follow them, you might just as well hand your dog tags to grave registration right now.

I mentioned we might like a house. Impossible, I was told. Who will stay in the house when you leave town? Who will answer the door for messengers and deliverymen? I said that I had lived in a house for twenty-four years in Los Angeles and had encountered the same problems. They were annoying, to be sure, but more than balanced by the advantages of householding, most specifically space. *You don't understand,* I was told, *it is different in New York.* A sentence, a caveat, used to end all argument. *It's different in New York. Sieg heil.* How different? I asked. Your house will be ripped off, a prognostication always followed by a hard, knowing little smile, as if the words "I told you so" had been stored, ready to be flung in my face the first time I dialed 911 to report a burglary at the house I had been warned not to buy. I said I had been burgled twice in Los Angeles. *You don't understand, it's different in New York.*

In fact, we bought an apartment rather than a house, not

because we yielded to the common wisdom but because it was in near move-in condition, the only place we could afford that was. It needed bookcases and a paint job and some new fixtures and the floors replaced, but that was about all. You don't know New York contractors, I was told. I know Los Angeles contractors, I replied. *You don't understand, it's different in New York.* I had the sense my instructors thought that contractors south of the Battery and west of the Hudson were bonded by St. Francis of Assisi. They lie about prices here and about how long the job's going to take, I was told. They lie in Los Angeles, I said, and I had the wound stripes to prove it; I had once threatened to strangle a carpenter who had glazed with glitter dust the bookcases he was meant to be painting a deep mauve. *Not like New York.* I said we wanted shutters in our dining room. Too expensive, I was told. In fact, the shutters I priced were cheaper than the last batch in Los Angeles. That was only the estimate, I was told. *You don't understand, it's different in New York.*

I could not keep a car. It would be stolen. The insurance was too expensive. There seemed a civic pride in this attitude, a reverse frontier ethic: New York is only for the hardy and the hearty, Beirut on the Hudson; anyone who lives anywhere else is only a petunia. It seemed uncharitable to point out that conspicuous consumption seemed to frame each of these arguments with which I was presented, that moving from the west side of Los Angeles to the east side of Manhattan was not exactly my definition of roughing it.

WE RENTED an industrial-size dumpster, with a nine-ton capacity, eighteen thousand pounds worth of one's life that would not make the cut and move with us to New York. A dumpster is a remarkably liberating piece of equipment. Having one parked in your driveway is like opening a psychological lock: it frees you to throw out the detritus of a spent and misspent life. The first weekend was euphoric, an orgasm of eliminating one's personal history, fifty-one file boxes into the dumpster—old tax returns, thirteen IRS audits, one of which came down to whether firewood was a deductible expense (we claimed the deduction because we heated an old house at the beach via a central fireplace; deduction denied), magazine expense accounts claiming meals with people I did not remember and whose names I probably invented, research for pieces that never came off, old newspaper clips ("A Search for a Nervous Indian"—a banner headline in the *San Francisco Examiner*, January 26, 1964, over a story about a "nervous, flat-featured young hitchhiker—possibly an American Indian" being sought as a possible murder suspect; my wife used the headline a dozen years later in a novel). The jetsam was a testament to how much I had learned in that quarter century, and how hard I had become in certain areas. Take, for example, the evolution in firing an agent. "This is more my fault than yours," began a four-page letter of dismissal in 1969; by the 1980s, alert to the beauties of the fax machine, I had come to favor the expeditious:

TO: Deborah Rogers
FROM: John Gregory Dunne
RE: Termination.

Please be advised that effective immediately Deborah Rogers and Rogers, Coleridge and White are terminated as the foreign representatives of John Gregory Dunne.

There were old yearbooks and high school literary magazines carrying short stories I had written, every one owing a debt to O. Henry, stories with titles like "The Deacon" (about a burglar who left a Bible at the site of each robbery, which of course he committed to pay for his invalid mother's hospitalization) and "Four Times Over" (about the father of quadruplets) and "Judgement" (about a doctor who justified an act of euthanasia with a quote from Hippocrates that I had come across in Bartlett's *Quotations:* "Extreme remedies are very appropriate for extreme diseases," Aphorisms, I, 6). "You are an asp in the bosom of the Catholic Church," the faculty adviser said when "Judgement" was presented to him, but he let the story be published. Even in my youth I was not terribly tolerant of criticism. "We have been much derided," I wrote in an editorial. "Self-appointed critics have taken it as their duty to ridicule us." This was a period in my life, I am embarrassed to say, when I was known as—no, when I called myself—J. Gregory Dunne. Nickname "Googs," another affect I apparently did nothing to discourage. *Me? Googs?* I had left a paper trail; I could not deny it.

"Googs—Anything I have said in this last and best year was all in fun," ran a note in my high school yearbook. "Poison Pen Peter begs forgiveness." For what? I could not remember. I did remember that as a going-away present I had bought him a piece of ass the night before he joined the Marine Corps and that fifteen years later he threw himself in front of a train. A bill dated 1 November 1960 from the Graben Hotel, Dorotheergasse 15, Vienna: was it there I had caught that dose of the clap, or at the Plaza Hotel, Knesebeckstrasse 15, in Berlin two days earlier? A week later in New York, pecker dripping, I had watched the election returns, Kennedy versus Nixon, at a black-tie party a woman I was seeing had invited me to, and I had to explain to her, no, we couldn't, I had a small problem of Teutonic origin. So do I, she said. She was in every way a freer spirit than I, dead now, a BMW belonging to a man not her husband wrapped around a tree, but nearly thirty years later, a question forms: Would she have told me had I not told her first?

There were copies of abusive letters, the kind I would write on days when I was blocked, when the work had come to a halt and I needed to get something, anything, on paper (to the CEO of American Express: "Dear Mr. Calvano: Perhaps you would think I owe you an explanation as to why I called Mr. Hardy in your Phoenix billing office a 'stupid fucking asshole' up whose anus I would like to shove my American Express card, #3793 007234 11004 . . .") and the mealy-mouthed responses these letters usually elicited (from James C. Calvano: "Dear Mr. Dunne: I must confess that I was taken aback by the tone of your letter, specifically your choice of language. It is my belief that courteous and professional service is the ultimate product we offer our cardholders . . .").

The mail I deposited into the dumpster was full of the most invidious criticism, sometimes even signed, usually from non-writers who mistook muscle-flexing invective for writing. Occasionally a professional felt impelled to flex his muscles: "Since I have enjoyed much of your writing, since I once met and spent the afternoon with you and your genius wife (your then baby child screaming in the other room) at a bad time in your lives when you were both poor and unknown and didn't know what to do about it (the man who brought us together was a fine gent named Collier Young)—*but most of all*, since I paid the dust-cover price of $18.95 for the book, I really feel I must tell you how I *despise The Red White and Blue*," ran one letter I received. The correspondent was a screenwriter with a number of good credits and we had indeed met, as he mentioned, just that once, nineteen years earlier.

"It is perhaps the most hate-filled, death-filled, contempt-for-humanity-filled work I have ever read. Céline wrote in the same anti-human spirit—but oh, his ugly words *sang* despite their despair. In your *Esquire* column on finishing the book, I felt so happy for you that the work was finally done. But you took all those years to write what—that it's all shit? For Christ sake, don't you think we know that?"

It seemed a nice mix between the abusive and the condescending, with the obligatory reference to "shit" that seems to invigorate so many screenwriters. I confess that my immediate inclination was to send him a condom with the instruction, "In this age of safe sex, it would be wise to roll this on before you go fuck yourself," but reason prevailed. My ultimate response was no less petty, small-minded and mean-spirited: "A novelist friend years ago gave me two pieces of sage advice—(1) never fuck a fan and (2) never engage in an argument with a correspondent. I have only the vaguest memory of any meeting with Collier Young. I know you used to be a hotshot screenwriter. That must be why Collier brought us together. The project came to naught. You were wearing leather."

I PORED OVER old daybooks, triggering forgotten memories. June 1970, Covington, Louisiana: "Drink with Walker Percy." Nothing more. My wife and I had spent that month crisscrossing the Deep South. The idea was not to speak to a single spokesman, to drink Dr Pepper at the general store and do the underwear and the dirty shirts at the crossroads coin laundry, to go to Little League games and get my hair cut while my wife got a manicure or a pedicure in the local beauty parlor—in other words, to take the pulse of the white South.

It was a patronizing notion; the piece was never written. And finally, in Covington, we relented on the spokesman idea, and called on Walker, a friend of a friend, but someone we had never met. We sat out in back by the bayou and drank whiskey and gin and tonics as a light rain fell. Walker never paid any attention to the rain, but just kept talking, pausing only to walk back up to the house to freshen up the drinks. Finally the skies parted, a thunderstorm, and still we sat outside and drank, watching the occasional water-skier on the black bayou water.

On the way back to New Orleans, on the Lake Pontchartrain causeway, my wife and I had a fight, ugly words, then silence. We spent the night at an airport motel, not speaking to each other, then took the 9:15 National flight to San Francisco the next morning, not exchanging a word until we got to the Hertz counter. I do not remember what the fight was about. Nor do I remember anything Walker had to say about the South. I do remember the sight of New Orleans coming up like a mirage at some point on the causeway, the gray water, the gray causeway, the gray skyline becoming one in the far distance, just about the time we lost sight of the shore behind us. And I remember something else about that month in the Deep South—the road glass. Whenever some member of the local gentry would pick us up to take us out to dinner, there would be a "road glass" on the dashboard, some spirits to fortify us for the ride to the local country club or the Holiday Inn dining room, martinis or a little straight whiskey with ice to tide us over. The ubiquitous road glass was the perfect pagan icon of the secular South.

.   .

EACH LOAD into the dumpster was like a stroll down memory lane, every piece of paper rich with nuance and the secrets of personal history. What I chose to keep was almost a dossier of loneliness. "Parties—Arnold & Tim—REgent 4-6344." A handwritten mimeographed flier that used to be passed out on the Upper East Side when I was first in New York after the army. "You're invited to our *Private PARTY*. Every Friday at 8:30 p.m. At our *Duplex Apartment* in a smart town house on 73 Street between 5th and Madison Avenues. These parties are *for Fun only*. Food and refreshments, Hi-Fi, music and lots of congenial people. In order to *balance* the fellows and gals we ask you to please telephone us any weekday after 6 p.m. for a reservation. Let us know if you are coming alone, with a date, or friends. $3 payable at the door to defray costs." And in the upper-left-hand corner: "Written up by Cue Magazine, November 9, 1957, etc., etc." Did I ever go to Arnold & Tim's? Or was I afraid to be one of the people who would?

A letter from Princeton: I had been named a distinguished alumnus, would I give a public lecture? I had not been back since the day I graduated (by the skin of my teeth), never paid my class dues, never gave a penny to the university; there is no classmate I see except by accident (a seatmate once on the Concorde from Paris). I searched my Princeton yearbook for clues; in my class poll, I was mentioned once, three votes in a category called "Summa cum Luncheon," or out to lunch. Clue enough. My senior thesis was in another box: "Lord Lothian—*Sero Sed Serio*." Philip Henry Kerr, eleventh marquess of Lothian (family motto *Sero Sed Serio*—Late, but in Earnest), one of the Cliveden set, an appeaser, but then appointed by Winston Churchill as ambassador to Washington in the early days of the war. The language was stilted, not so much mock academic as mock graduate student. "Philip Henry Kerr," read the first sentence, "was born on April 18, 1882, into an emblazoned background of a noble and aristocratic heritage." I skipped a hundred pages to the peroration:

> His was a life that spanned the achievements, the failures, the disillusion of two eras, each in mutual antagonism with the other. For the greater part of his adulthood he was unable to reconcile the two. But in the brief space of sixteen months, when the fate of the free world hung on the brink of catastrophe, he stabilized and added depth to his opinions, and presented his country's case with such force and judgment that the survival of democratic civilization was assured.

That shit was worth an A (and was the only reason I was allowed to graduate). Years later, prior to that same trip where I picked up my venereal souvenir, I sent a copy of the thesis to the twelfth marquess, whose address I found in Debrett's. I was callow enough to think it might garner an invitation to a weekend at the ancestral home. It did not. I hope it was not because he read it.

Of course I had accepted the invitation to Princeton. Who would miss the opportunity to return as a distinguished visitor to a place where he had been so unhappy? I have never trusted those who look fondly back on their college years as the happiest in their lives; it seems the definition of arrested development. The undergraduate, caught in that limbo between adolescence and adulthood, is meant to be unhappy if he has any hint of intelligence. I had belonged to one of the better eating clubs, but only because the club desired my roommate, who was later voted Most Likely to Succeed in my class (and did not); I was assured a position, but was asked not to sign the bicker book until later in the evening; the inference I drew was that other names were more likely to attract stellar classmates.

Five days on campus, with posters in every entryway heralding my presence, and I found myself sinking into the same slough of despond in which I swam as an undergraduate. My wife had never been to Princeton before, and the campus scratched in her that western populism that never lies far beneath the surface, even when camouflaged by a Chanel suit and a mink coat. This is the architecture of entitlement, she said, as we strolled under the archways of the faux-Gothic buildings. You will never understand power in America until you come to a campus like this. At a land grant college—she had gone to Berkeley—such buildings would be meant for public use, for libraries and laboratories, not to provide private rooms for spoiled undergraduates. She warmed to her rhetoric. Princeton is not a university, she said. It's an academic theme park—Ivy Land.

The memories overwhelmed; I could not disagree. At an urban campus, there is access to a real world; in the rural fastness of Princeton, the students are left to contemplate what they seem to accept as their own moral imperative; the undergraduate years are only a prelude to a life of anticipated achievement. I spoke to my class; three people I had hardly known as a student confided to me that they had been recently fired. I never really got beyond middle management at the bank, said one. Another spoke of relocating "to the Tampa area" and of the opportunities he had found there in residential real estate after . . . after the people who bought his family business unloaded him. I have my health, said the third, and my grandchildren. That's wonderful, really terrific, that's what counts. None of us said that the joy of relocating to the Tampa area had not been part of the Princeton bargain.

• •

THE PRINCETON posters went into the dumpster. A thousand
pounds, two thousand, then ten. I was like the drowning man
whose life is said to flash before his eyes. The documentation
of my youth was there. I had not wanted so much to write,
as to have written, to be a writer, a published writer. I thought
there were shortcuts, that to write down a story idea ("Com-
munist political official meets and seduces exiled duchess at
film festival; contracts syphilis") was to write the story. There
were dozens of such ideas, one scratched on the back of a grocery bag: "American couple in Europe look up child sired by
man during war and find him pimping for his mother." Many
of the ideas had to do with writers ("Successful writer invited
to dinner by an old love & her new husband, and is drunkenly
accused by the husband of writing about his affair with wife in
last novel"); "successful novelist," "successful screenwriter,"
"successful playwright," again "successful writer," and again,
and again, psycho-history on the march.

There was a will, but no way. Among the papers I had squir-
reled away, I found a perfectly worked-out idea for a novel
that I have no memory of ever starting, this from that time of
innocence when I thought fiction could be plotted and out-
lined in advance. "The three main characters in this book are
Walter Dublin, thirty-three, a Paris-based European correspondent for a newspaper and magazine empire," I had written
(when? probably I was still in my twenties, when I thought
thirty-three an impossibly glamorous age); "his wife Zab
(Elizabeth), twenty-nine, a French doctor" (I remember Zab;
it was a name I had seen in Igor Cassini's Cholly Knicker-
bocker column; Zab meant exotic and erotic; there were no
Zabs in Hartford, not in the Junior League and definitely not

at St. Justin's parish); "and Walter's brother Daniel J. (called 'Deej' because he thinks Dan 'a stage Mick name'), a homosexual Broadway stage director now making television commercials." The outline had the fascination of a snake. "Basically the story is about three people's discovery of each other and their coming to terms with the personalities beneath the thin veneer." What thin veneer? Walter was "brutally frank about his shallowness. He married Zab knowing she was mortally ill with leukemia." And Zab? "Being a doctor she suspects her condition." Back to Walter: "Toward Zab, he feels if not love a real affection. There are times however when he dreams of her funeral and the marvelous cloak of pity in which he can wrap himself, receiving the regrets, etc. Thus Walter is a strange mixture." And finally: "This book will look at shallow people, bored and sterile people, who know what they are and whose only solution is to make the best they can of what they have, people who, as Walter says, 'don't have the energy to be unhappy.'"

As if moving were not bad enough for the quinquagenarian (or the "quink," as I had taken to calling those in my age bracket), I was also being forced to confront the pretensions and the absurdities of the stranger the quink once was.

INTERNAL AFFAIRS INVESTIGATION (*cont'd*)

Q: You mentioned psycho-history. Isn't that what this was?
A: Of course. I said it was.
Q: With the dumpster a convenient metaphor?
A: Convenient. But it was there.
Q: The dumpster held nine tons of refuse. Are you trying to say all eighteen thousand pounds came under the heading of psycho-history?

A: You could say that anything has meaning to somebody.

Q: But you did pick and choose?

A: My material, my rules.

Q: Then did you plan it to make a point?

A: My material, my rules.

Q: Are you Walter Dublin?

A: That hurt.

Q: Are you?

A: That was thirty years ago. I hope to Christ not now.

Q: So. You've made a meal out of your cardiac adventure and another out of moving; you don't have that much more to play with.

A: Roots. There's nothing like a cardiac adventure to make one want to return to his roots.

Q: Frog Hollow?

A: Farther back. Ireland. I'd never been there. But first Germany. I grew up in Germany.

PART FOUR

XIII

Six A.M. I was taking the night flight to Frankfurt. From there to Wertheim and my old army *kaserne*. Up at dawn as usual and into the park, sweat clothes and a brisk walking pace, three miles in forty-two minutes, pulse rate up, heart pounding. Good for the ticker? It won't hurt, the cardiologist replied. My new New York cardiologist. Not a man to commit himself. The only WASP internist in Manhattan (my joke). He wears pink Brooks Brothers shirts with a hairline stripe and calls me "Pal" or "Chief" or sometimes "Sport." I call him Tim. For every minute of exercise you do, Tim says, you'll probably live a minute longer. I do some elementary math. Forty-two minutes a day; say forty-five, three-quarters of an hour. Three hundred days a year (365 days less bad-weather days, travel days, sick days—not hangover days; hangover days I force myself out at dawn; penance), three-quarters of an hour a day, that's 225 hours a year, divided by the 24 hours in a day, that's nine extra days of life per year; in forty years I'll have logged in enough hours to add an extra year; it makes you wonder about exercise, all that sweating and grunting, all those hi-tech shoes and pulse meters and expensive

149

exercise sweats, and the Walkman to get you through the boredom, Jim Morrison belting out "Waiting for the Sun" and other golden oldies that make you feel not quite so past it, so middle-fucking-aged. Does it make you feel good, Sport? Yes, I say. Then do it. The gospel according to Tim.

Out of the park for a bialy and some freshly squeezed OJ at a little hole-in-the-wall on Sixth Avenue. The blue Volvo sedan was parked on the east side of Sixth at the corner of Central Park South, by the St. Moritz Hotel. It looked as if it had been run through a trash compactor. The roof on the right side, the curb side, was caved in, the windshield smashed and splattered with blood. I thought for a moment that the Volvo had been sideswiped by a truck, but the street side of the car was undamaged, as was the hood. Something had obviously crashed into it from above. I looked toward the roof of the St. Moritz. "A jumper," said the cop who suddenly materialized at my side. He made a gesture simulating a swan dive. "Off the roof." I tried to triangulate the angle of the fall. There were several setbacks on the higher floors of the hotel, and then there was the sidewalk, maybe fifteen feet wide at that point. I would have thought a body would fall straight down, probably catching one of the lower setbacks. He—or she—must have pushed off with enormous strength to make the Volvo. I noticed that the Volvo had New Jersey plates.

This was my second New York jumper. Ten years earlier, I was getting out of a cab in front of the Yale Club on Vanderbilt Avenue when a jumper landed in the street just behind the taxi. It never made the papers. As it happened, my wife was having her picture taken the following day by a *Daily News* photographer. I asked why there had been no mention of the suicide in the newspapers, no picture of the crumpled body lying in the middle of Vanderbilt Avenue. "You got to catch a jumper in the air to make the paper," the photographer said. It seemed a reasonable enough explanation at the time, especially as it implied an epidemic of defenestrations. I remembered still another, the troubled daughter of an actress I knew slightly in Los Angeles, from an apartment building just off Sunset Boulevard. It was Easter Sunday. She had left a note for her mother: "Happy Easter." It seemed the most awful kind of suicide. With pills, you can at least change your mind, reach for the telephone; with a gun, the trigger could remain unpulled, and if pulled, death before the noise even reaches the ears. The jumper cannot change his mind, and it's a long way down.

The Volvo had been towed away by the time I went to the airport. In the TWA lounge, I found the story buried, no bylines, in the late editions with the Wall Street closings. The victim was Swiss, only twenty-five, a businessman from Zurich. He had jumped from an upper floor of the St. Moritz after checking into a room on the sixth floor. He had written suicide notes—plural—in German, which had been translated into English by officials from the Swiss consulate, which had been notified of the incident; the contents of the notes were not revealed. He went from his room on the sixth floor to the thirty-third floor, where he jumped. His body was found at 4:55 A.M. He had removed his glasses and his wristwatch before jumping. It was not said who discovered the body, nor was the owner of the Volvo with the New Jersey license plates identified.

I CANNOT SLEEP on planes, nor can I watch the movie. I also find it difficult to read, and I have never been an easy communicant, if I am traveling alone, with my seatmate. I would like to think I could converse easily with the flight attendants (who, in simpler times, used to be called stewardesses), but there is something about air travel that conjures up for me priapic fantasies of the most breathtaking permutations, so that always, when I ask the stewardess what her turnaround time is in Frankfurt (and yes, don't mind if I do have another glass, I like zinfandel, don't you, Oh, you like the cabernets, I like them, too, I'm a real cabernet man), there lurks just behind my crooked smile that real conversation stopper, "Let's fuck." This is why now, whenever I travel, I bring a battery-operated laptop computer with me, saltpeter for the daydream of getting it on with "Hi, I'm Patti" in the first-class can. So: TWA 740, JFK–Frankfurt, had hardly cleared New York air traffic control before I opened my Toshiba 1000 and created the file "Jumper."

"QUESTIONS," I wrote.
1. Why did he take off his watch and glasses?
    What kind of watch? Rolex?
    What kind of glasses? Ralph Lauren?
2. Why more than one suicide note?
    Who to? He was only 25. Parent & girl/boy
    friend? Was he doing anything illegal?

Patti passed the zinfandel. Crooked smile at the ready, I asked how many full fares in first class. Zip, she said. Everyone's an upgrade. I guess you see a lot of that now, I said. Companies don't send executives first class now, Patti said. They've got so many frequent-flier miles they don't have to. They just upgrade. Heavy nod: I hadn't thought of that. A little more of that zinfandel. A quick leer: if you don't mind.

Down lights. The in-flight feature was a Steve Martin movie. I opened the laptop again. I wrote:

WHAT IF THIS WERE THE STORY:

The victim was a woman. She was a young call girl. The man was from out of town, staying at the St. Moritz. Someone had given him the girl's number. Or perhaps he took the telephone number from an escort service advertised on that late-night TV public-access channel, the one where the naked bald fat guy talks with a lot of naked bookkeepers with bad teeth and droopy boobs about what makes them hot, Channel 23. He had called the service, the one doing all the commercials that night, Quality Misses, and the service had picked up on the first ring and arranged to send the girl over. She had arrived at 4:30 A.M. She seemed nice, attractive, and was wearing a mink coat. She said her name was Charlie. She said Charlie was short for Charlotte. She said it was all right if he paid her after they were finished. She said for him to go into the bathroom to get ready. She asked if he minded wearing a condom. He said he would prefer it. She said she liked her hotel clients to wear pajamas because she thought it was comfortable if they undressed from pajamas. She had brought a nightgown with her. This whole scenario really appealed to him. She opened her bag and laid out a black nightgown on the bed. She said he should brush his teeth and wash his mouth out with Scope and she would be ready when he got out of the bathroom. He saw her remove a fresh packet of Ramses from her bag and place it on the bedside table. Hurry up, she said. She had dropped her mink coat on the chair by the window. There were French doors leading to the small terrace. She opened the curtains leading to the terrace, and then the doors. The night air made the curtains billow. He went into the bathroom. He put on his pajamas and his bathrobe and his slippers. He rinsed his mouth with Scope and sprayed on some Givenchy cologne. He tried not to think of his wife and children. Then he came out of the bathroom.

Curaçao? A little Rémy? Patti was holding a tray of liqueurs. Kahlúa?

A little Kahlúa on the rocks might hit the spot. Two. One for me, one for thee.

A dazzling Patti smile. I'm a working girl, that's a no-no.

Say, what's your turnaround time in Frankfurt?

And why do you want to know that?

An insistent call light from seat 3A. Miss, I need a pillow, that man has two.

Ciao.

She was not there. Her mink coat was still on the chair. The condoms were on the bedside table. Her black nightgown was lying across the bed. Her purse was on the chair. For a moment he thought she might be on the terrace. He said Charlie. But when he went out on the terrace she was not there either. In the distance he heard a siren but did not connect it to her. He felt a sense of unease. He went to the door, opened it, looked down the corridor, but there was no one there. He did not know where she was. Or why she had left the room, leaving her mink coat and her purse behind. He checked the closets. Perhaps she was playing Hide & Go Seek. He went to the open terrace again. It was now getting chilly. He looked down. And then his heart sank. He saw the people gathering below, on Sixth Avenue. He knew immediately what had happened. Did she fall? Did she jump?

Mid-Atlantic. All lights out. Patti was curled up in an empty seat just past the galley. Michelle was on duty. Michelle looked as if she had been working for TWA since Howard Hughes's time. Michelle had mileage. Back to the computer.

He wondered if the police could figure out the room she had

jumped from. Or would they claim she was pushed? He could hardly breathe. They would check the trajectory. She could only have jumped from an 05 room, because each 05 room had a terrace, and from the terrace she would have hit the street, where if she had jumped from a room with just a window and no terrace she would have hit the sidewalk. He wondered if he should get dressed and leave and pretend he had not been in the room. But her coat was there, and her nightgown and her purse. And the escort service would know she had been sent to room 3105 at the St. Moritz. How long would it take to identify her? He checked her bag. There were two credit cards, Diners and Amex, both in the name of C. A. Moran. A charge slip from Bloomingdale's for some lingerie, made out to C. A. Moran; my God, he thought, could it be that nightgown? What else? $192 in cash and some silver, a hairbrush, some loose condoms, a diaphragm, basic cosmetics—lipstick, mascara, eyebrow pencil—a charge card for the Lenox Hill Hospital Health Care Center made out to C. A. Moran, some Kleenex, a handkerchief, a container of spermicidal foam, an address book, a diary. He looked at the last entry in the diary. It was undated, written in a precise hand. The last sentence was: "My cunt has been my meal ticket for almost seven years. A woman who makes her living from her cunt is lazy, without self-respect, self-destructive. I am not stupid, but only stupid women live by their cunt. I must take charge. What can I do with the rest of my life? My cunt will not be young forever. . . ."

First light. Landfall below. Probably Ireland. I would be there in a week.

The entry nearly made him ill. He had given the escort service his real name, because he was of course registered in room

3105, and the drill was that the service called back, as had the girl, and the hotel operator would not have rung him had they just asked for a room. He should have said his name was Kennedy and he was meeting someone in room 3105 after a business dinner and an evening at Mickey Mantle's down the street. He put the diary back into her purse. He wondered what to do with the nightgown. Where had she kept it? It would not fit into the bag. He picked up her mink coat. Carol & Mary, Honolulu, it said. Who would buy a mink coat in Honolulu? There was an inside pocket attached to the lining. That must be where she put it. He wondered about C. A. Moran when he heard the voices coming down the corridor. He waited for the knock at the door.

Patti: "This concludes the audio portion of the flight. Please pass your headsets to the aisle, where a flight service attendant will collect them. . . ."

QUESTIONS:
1. Why is he staying at the St. Moritz?
   What is his business and how will this incident affect it?
2. Who is C. A. Moran?
   Where does she come from?
   Why is she a hooker?
3. Who owns the Volvo that C. A. Moran had smashed into?
   What is a Volvo with Jersey plates doing parked on Sixth Avenue at 5 A.M. Something illicit?
   Perhaps the owner is philandering and now he is caught as well as the man in room 3105.
   Is there a registration in the car?
   If not, do the police check the license plate and call the party to whom the car is registered?

Who is this party and how does this situation affect him?

The same sense of suffocating paranoia.

4. Could C. A. Moran have landed on a homeless person and killed him/her when she jumped?

This gets the press on the case.

5. Or interrupted a robbery in process by landing on the person robbing the blue Volvo?

Patti again: "It has been our pleasure to serve you. . . ." Patti then did it in German. Patti had facets I had not imagined. "Well, you must have some big meeting today, the way you worked all night," Patti said at the exit. "Good luck." *Guten tag*, Patti.

INTERNAL AFFAIRS INVESTIGATION (*cont'd*):

Q: Would a hooker really be wearing a mink coat?
A: The streetwalkers do on Sixth Avenue. Mainly because they're working the hotels in the area, so it's upmarket. I suppose they get the coats from their pimps. And those girls on the escort service commercials on Channel 23 are always dressed as if they're going to a charity ball.
Q: Do you watch Channel 23 much?
A: They didn't have anything like that in Los Angeles.
Q: That's a nonresponsive answer.
A: I watch it occasionally.
Q: Don't you think C. A. Moran is sentimental?
A: Yes.
Q: Is that why you didn't do anything with it?
A: No. That can be fixed. It's the situation the man finds himself in that is interesting, the way he is trapped.
Q: So why didn't you do anything with it?

A: Because essentially all it is really is a movie situation. And at that, only the opening of a movie. The first reel.

Q: Will you ever do anything with it?

A: I just did.

XIV

I CRASHED for a day at a hotel in Frankfurt before renting a car for the drive to Wertheim. There was a Bible in the bedside table, with a bookmark of sorts stuck in it, a pornographic playing card, the nine of hearts, a young woman giving head to one faceless man and masturbating another. The bookmark was in I *Könige*—Kings—and I jotted down the citation at the top of the page—chapter XI, verses 1–43—so that I might look it up in an English-language Bible when I returned home. Relevant stuff, it turned out: "But King Solomon loved many strange women, together with the daughter of Pharaoh, women of the Moabites, Ammonites, Edomites, Zidonians and Hittites." Strange Moabite women doing unto Solomon what the nine of hearts was doing unto her masters. I finally dozed off, a troubled, revved-up, jet-lagged sleep, shards of dreams competing with each other, Patti occupying pride of place, Patti on the return flight across the Atlantic kibitzing my game of porno solitaire, fellatio jack of diamonds on cunnilingus queen of spades, buggery deuce of clubs on red double-decker trey, perhaps a lesbian joker filling in for the missing nine of hearts.

Midafternoon. Fitfully awake. The hotel TV carried CNN via satellite. Lying under the quilt on my bed, I cleaned my fingernails with the nine of hearts while watching reports on the California primary. Minicams in Silicon Valley, sound bites from Nickerson Gardens in Watts. The marvel of modern communications. In the studio, Robert Novak huffed, Patrick Buchanan puffed. Fred Barnes here, Morton Kondracke there, Michael Kinsley holding up the progressive end. I decided, not for the first time, that I detested politics. And politicians more than politics. And the main-chancers who work for politicians more than the politicians themselves. But most of all I detested those people I was staring at on the tube, the op-ed grandees who moonlight as talking heads, that symbiotic army of the knowing who would explain the political process to us, at least as they wish us to believe it functions. See them on the Sunday talk shows, this Brinkley, that Broder, see them on CNN. Jerked off by the main-chancers and loving it to the last drop. "Plump" is the word that fits them best. They are plump of body, plump of mind, the cholesterol of smarm and self-importance clogging every mental artery, bloated bladders of hot air farting the most noxious kind of knowingness out through the cathode-ray tube. They have nothing to tell me, these Kondrackoids of the process, they have nothing to tell any of us about the United States of America. Clarity came six thousand miles from campaign central at the Century Plaza, and with clarity at last a dreamless sleep, with fury abated.

NOTES WRITTEN IN A LOUSY ITALIAN RESTAURANT IN FRANKFURT:

1. Why is the judgment "He does not suffer fools gladly" always taken as a compliment? In my experience, it is usually said to excuse someone for being an unpleasant

prick. Anyway, fools are gold. Also: a lot of shits are called "perfectionists" as a way to justify their being shits. It's possible to do a riff on that.

2. Why does German architecture remind me of strudel?
3. Why do so many German men wear ankle-length black leather Panzer coats? *Kristallnacht* coats. *Sieg heil* coats.
4. How do you write a sympathetic character who leaves a pornographic playing card in a hotel Bible?
5. Incidental information: *C* and *S* are the only two letters in the alphabet to have separate volumes in the twelve-volume OED. *S* in fact has two volumes to itself. Something to play with.
6. Re J's call from L.A. She's covering the California primary. J says P was on the press bus. P is an actress and political groupie we've known forever. "She still has that insane glitter in her eye," J said. "It comes from trying to remember who she hasn't fucked," I said. J said P was fucking a senior member of So-and-so's campaign this trip out. P had also reported to J that this was the first time she had ever really been in love.
7. How do I deal with J? Is it too coy to just call her "J" or "Joan" or "my wife"? No other ID. I think so. She dislikes being considered as part of a couple as much as I do. Too much mileage on that construct.
8. Headline from the *International Herald Tribune:*
   VIRGINIA AIR CONDITIONS DEATH CHAMBER
   Could be useful.

RICHMOND, VA. (UPI)—The Corrections Department is air-conditioning the state penitentiary's death chamber to make it "more comfortable for everybody," it was reported today.

No sweat.

• •

AT THE HERTZ counter in Frankfurt, the only car with an automatic transmission was a Volvo sedan with Swiss plates. Just like the baby on Sixth Avenue. Even the same color blue. Pasadena, I said to the Hertz clerk. Pasadena, California, she said, very, very slowly, as if she were wondering how to compute the pickup charge from Pasadena back to Frankfurt and then on to Bern. No, Pasadena means I pass, I said. Pass? she said. *Amerikanische* slang, I said. Movie slang. *Kine* slang. *Verstehen* Twentieth Century–Fox? My GI German was still operative. *Verstehen* Barry Diller? She did not *verstehen* Barry Diller. It means *finito*, I said. *Nicht* Volvo. I'd had my Volvo experience that week; I'd pay the extra DMs and take the BMW with the stick shift.

Frankfurt to Wertheim, making tracks, 140 kilometers an hour; less than cruising speed on the autobahn. The Germans passed as if they were invading Belgium once again. Up on your tail, really riding it, this was at almost 90 miles an hour, and then their headlights were blinking, blitzkrieg, Brussels by lunch to accept the surrender. In the rearview mirror, I could see a fat burgher with fingers like jelly rolls waving me over into the slow lane. Up went the bird. Sit on this, *Herr Oberstleutnant*, and rotate.

Off the autobahn at Marktheidenfeld, through villages that had the familiarity of dreamscapes. Outside Altfeld, a U.S. Army convoy was parked along the side of the road. At the head of the column there was an accident, a jeep in a ditch, a German honey wagon—used to transport manure—on its side, the usual military balls-up: a half-colonel apoplectic, an MP trying to reroute traffic. A sudden memory of the paperwork a military accident entailed. Personal experience. Nineteen fifty-six, an alert. We had combat readiness alerts every month. The alert orders came down from Seventh Army in Heidelberg, any hour of the day or night, New Year's Eve, Fourth of July, remember Pearl Harbor, and within an hour every unit in the command had to be packed and off post, meeting up at predesignated staging areas so the generals would know how long it would take to deploy in case Russian tanks actually were rolling in from Czechoslovakia. In those days it was thought Seventh Army would last about thirty-six hours if it was the real thing, which gave every alert a certain piquant quality. In the personnel section—I was the personnel clerk for Baker Battery—every form, every mimeographed order, every morning report, every personnel and medical record, every bound regulation (the ARs and the SRs, they were called; the ARs were army regulations, the SRs standard, or military regulations) had to be loaded onto the deuce-and-a-half we had been allocated, along with our typewriters and our weapons. If war came I was armed with an M-1 and a Royal Standard; I think thirty-six hours was an optimistic assessment of my remaining life-span.

On the road, 4 A.M., the battalion rumbling through tiny Bavarian villages rich with the smell of honey wagons and cow shit. A crossroads. The truck behind our deuce-and-a-half, its load out of balance, took the turn too sharply and rolled over. The PFC riding in the shotgun seat was a badass from the big empty. His name was Arnold and he was richly decorated with tattoos. My favorite was the watch around his wrist; the watch band was a snake, the face a death head, the numbers drops of blood. In his version, Arnold's life was one continuous brush with the law, with appropriate scenarios in which he had escaped capture for felonies unmentioned. The best way to get rid of a mororcycle cop on your tail, he had told me, was to drop a railroad tie out of your car into the cop's path. I had once worked on the railroad—a college-type summer job—and I was dubious, but Arnold was not the kind of person to whom you said, Arnold, a railroad tie weighs a hundred pounds, and what's it doing in the back of your car anyway, it's covered with creosote, and it won't fit. The tattooed snake on his wrist tended to discourage argument. When Arnold Rausch said it was beautiful to see a motorcycle cop hit that tie, that motherfucker wished he had wings, him going one way and his motorcycle—Arnold always pronounced it "motorsickle"—going another, it was best to say, Hey, Arnold, beautiful.

Arnold had dropped his last railroad tie. His neck was broken. A medic was trying to extract his tongue so he would not swallow it. On the roadbed, the chaplain was laying out the oils for extreme unction to give Arnold the last rites. The battalion personnel officer, a jaunty little CWO3, who had last been assigned to an airborne division, bounced out of our truck to take a look. He had over a hundred jumps to his credit and he was always telling paratrooper stories, just to let us know what a candyass outfit he thought the artillery was, you don't know what hash looks like until you see a Roman candle, his chute don't open, splat, corn beef hash, crack an egg, drop it on the bastard, you could spoon him up for chow. He seemed disappointed that Arnold didn't look like hash.

"Get the ARs and the SRs," the personnel officer shouted up at me. "AR Form 88 dash 9021, Death by Vehicular Accident." The chaplain seemed embarrassed. "He's not dead yet," he whispered. Arnold was trying to nod in agreement. "You better say the words quick, Padre," the personnel officer said. "He's not going to be around to hear the end, you don't move it."

I pulled the relevant ARs and SRs, the AR Form 88 dash 9021, and Arnold's 201 file from the cabinets stored on the truck. In my heart of hearts, I knew it was going to be easier to fill out the forms if Arnold was still alive.

"Hi, Arnold."

There was a flicker of eye movement.

"You were born March the eighteenth, nineteen thirty-six, right?"

Tears had begun to well in Arnold's eyes.

"No next of kin?" Foundling hospital, foster homes, state training school, IQ 92—an entire history of the American underclass could be written from GI 201 files.

The medic said, "Jesus fucking Christ."

The chaplain said, "Is he Catholic?"

"Padre, we don't know if this is the real thing or not," the personnel officer said. It was as if he was hoping that Russki armor was rolling in from Czecho. "Just say something. We got to bag him and get him off the road." To me he said: "Ask him who loaded the truck."

It did not seem an entirely appropriate question to ask a dying man.

"There's got to be a statement of charges against whoever loaded that truck," the personnel officer said with some exasperation. "That's military property, someone's going to have to pay. If it's him, we'll charge it to his death benefits. AR Form 902 slash 12—Change of Beneficiary."

The chaplain said, "I will go unto the altar of God . . .."

"Arnold, who helped you load the truck?"

It was the last question Arnold Rausch ever heard.

•   •

In a way, Arnold Rausch was the reason I was returning to Wertheim and Peden Barracks. For thirty years I had, however unwittingly, made my living off the army. Had I not been drafted, I almost surely would have remained what I had become—the quintessential Princeton prig. What the service had provided was an exit visa from the stalag of the middle class into the terra incognita of the culturally and economically stateless, that hardscrabble patch where I had mined so much of my material. It was not so much that I wished to embrace that life; it was that it changed the way I thought about my own. If I had not gone into the army as an enlisted man, if I had not experienced what it was like to be a have-not, with the have-not's almost palpable distrust of the haves, I doubt that I ever would have been so professionally drawn to outsiders. I conceived of my return to Wertheim, after thirty-two years, as a sentimental journey, a reunion as it were at the informal institution where I had received my higher education, a doctorate in the meaner aspects of life. The adventure was, of course, a literary conceit, a psychic treasure hunt: I was going back to Peden Barracks so that I could write about going back, a man in his fifties who, after glimpsing some real or imagined void, would try to find clues to explain how he had become what he had become. In other words, I would watch myself watching. I had, however, failed to consider the absolute in the construct: a sentimental journey is by definition sentimental.

I stayed in a new tennis hotel outside Wertheim, indoor and outdoor courts, one star in the *Guide Michelin*. It appeared the perfect spot for weekend trysting, a judgment reinforced at lunch in the restaurant, where old men with muscle tone, their parchment skin a shiny tanning-studio brown, fondled young women I would have wagered were not their wives.

That afternoon, I left my car on the quay beside the Main and wandered through the streets of the town, examining the half-timbered houses in the *marktplatz* as I had never done when I was a GI. Wertheim is no more distinguished than a hundred other small medieval cities in Germany, its main claim for attention being that it is old. On the promontory dominating the town rise the red ruins of a feudal Gothic castle, and it was there I stopped on my way to the *kaserne*. Wertheim hunkered below in the confluence of the Main and the Tauber rivers; in the distance, the horizon was broken by the Odenwald and the dark wooded heights of the Spessart. Here was another view I had missed as a PFC. Already I had the uneasy feeling that I was overindulging that middle-aged longing for an epiphany, this after a lifetime's rejection of parables and epiphanies, not to mention the secrets locked in the majesty of landscape.

Peden Barracks was just up the hill from the castle. Except for some new dependent housing just outside the base perimeter, nothing seemed to have changed; it looked like a place I had visited only last Thursday. Over the main gate was the emblem of the 72d Field Artillery Brigade, the same command as when I had been stationed there thirty years before. "On Time, On Target" was the brigade's motto, and it occurred to me suddenly that the motto had a somewhat tentative, problematic quality; it was less swaggering certainly than "First to Fight," less unrelenting than "Neither Fear Nor Favor," and it seemed more appropriate to the annual fund-raising drive at Our Lady of Perpetual Help R.C. Church than to cannoneers on the march. Thoroughly miserable in the teeming rain, the guard at the gate was in full combat gear—M-16, barrel down to keep it dry, poncho over camouflage fatigues,

and the new military steel pot, with the configuration of the
World War II Wehrmacht helmet, high over the eyes, flanged
at the sides and in the back. I found the helmet acutely dis-
turbing, its design displaying a certain historical insensitivity.
However practical and protective the helmet might be, the
Brits and the French did not deck their grunts out to look like
the Waffen SS, and I wondered why we thought it necessary.

It was still pouring the next morning when I was waved
onto the post. I appeared to have the status of visiting digni-
tary, although none of the officers at brigade headquarters gave
any evidence of knowing or caring what I was supposed to be
dignified for, other than that I had once served at Peden in
some previous incarnation, an old fart who could just as well
have been a retired VFW post commander come to bore them
to death about the good old days when the caissons really did
hit the dusty trail. Had I been an officer or an EM? What was
the designation of my old unit? My MOS? Howitzers or guns?
Self-propelled or motor-drawn? The questions were never
asked. Nor was I asked to produce any identification or credentials or list any credits to prove I was who I said I was; I had
not expected so relaxed an attitude toward security, especially
with the Germans still touchy about American missile systems
on German soil.

My contact was the deputy community commander at the
kaserne, a lieutenant colonel, formerly a paratrooper with the
82d Airborne, now an administrator in the Quartermaster
Corps in charge of the post's military and civilian support bureaucracy. Over his office door there was a photograph of John
Wayne in the camouflage fatigues he had worn in *The Green
Berets*. I was too polite a guest to mention that John Wayne
seemed an unlikely and unmartial role model for an officer on

the first line of the nation's defense; for all his Commie-bashing and soundstage heroics, the Duke had never served the colors he professed to honor so much. Image versus reality, with the Duke neither on time nor on target.

As I pondered the photograph, I suddenly realized what I should have known instinctively when I undertook this journey: returning to Wertheim was like retaking a course I had already passed with honors. I would experience no new epiphanies; there were no untapped memories, no unanswered questions. There was only the army, so new and vivid and dangerous and unexpected when I was twenty-two, an institution predicated on the economic and social determinism of rank having its privileges, with all the concomitant factors, affecting officers as well as enlisted men—the low pay, the backwater bases, the grubbing after perks and goodies, the sullen wives ever resentful at having to live in housing rather than houses, with scarcely an inch of beaverboard separating them from the family fractures in the quarters next door. The army was constant; except cosmetically, nothing had really changed. Sociologically the army's place in the nation's cultural equation is suggested by a single fact: the enlisted army is the only major institution in American life in which blacks have more years of education than whites. This was a subject the officers in a line unit were not prepared to address, nor were the questions asked by a writer whose vision was tunneled on his own fragile psyche.

Instead I found only the ironies and the reportorial fill to which a professional writer is almost tropistically attracted. As I walked through the barracks, it was quite apparent that the white enlisted ranks were still drawn from that segment of society where the tattoo is the most relevant of the pictorial arts; I noticed snakes and griffins and Satan and satyrs and tits and pudenda and odes to mother and country and snatch, dark Rorschach representations never seen on the television commercials ("We're Army . . . Navy . . . Air Force . . . Marines") pushing enlistment in the military. The tattoos reminded me of a story I had clipped earlier that year from the *Miami Herald*, about a U.S. Navy warship on patrol in the Persian Gulf. The vessel evoked this society complete; nightly AA meetings were held in the sick bay, and only three sailors at a time were permitted in the ship's PX, each stripped to his skivvies to cut down shoplifting. As with the navy, so the army.

Many of the officers on post, including the CO of Headquarters Company in the service battalion, were women. In theory, there are no women in combat units, but in a theater like Europe, where war, if it breaks out, is only moments away, every support unit is in effect a combat outfit, making the distinction academic. My old room in the barracks, the room in which my two roommates, the clerk and the cannoneer, had fondled each other in the dark, was now the office of the woman company commander. Dutifully I copied the sign on the wall: "Don't Criticize the Coffee. You'll Be Old and Weak One Day Yourself." Everywhere there was the peculiar military assault on the language. Outside one latrine, a sign read: "Be a Believer. The Hostile Threat to USAREUR OPSEC Is Real." I asked an officer to translate. USAREUR was U.S. Army Europe; OPSEC was operational security. But what did it mean? "Well," he said, "we don't want our personnel going into town and talking about the kind of exercises their units are going on." I suggested that the reality of the threat to USAREUR OPSEC might be more effectively conveyed by something punchier, on the order of "Loose Lips Sink

Ships." The reference was unfamiliar to him, which made me feel even more superannuated.

What struck me that day was how middle-class the military always tries to appear, all evidence to the contrary, to the civilian visitor. On my guided tour of the base, the emphasis was not on the military gear and the lethal weaponry—the self-propelled gun and multiple-launch rocket battalions, the Patriot air defense missile battery—but on the new preschool and the library and the gym and the weight room and the Rod & Gun Club. I was told about the exemplary community relations between the *kaserne* and the town of Wertheim and I was told about the number of dependent wives who worked in the post economy as teachers and preschool attendants. It reminded me of the way people in Las Vegas talked about their churches and schools, as if faith and education were the city's main attractions rather than gambling and fucking.

Egalitarianism prevailed. There was even a duty roster for bus monitor; every officer and enlisted man who had a child in the dependents' high school in Wurzburg, some twenty miles away, was on it, including the executive officer of the brigade, a light colonel, whose daughter was a high school junior. His name was Kelly and he had been stationed on the post for five years, two years longer than the normal tour in the European theater, assigned first as brigade operations officer and then recently promoted to XO. The 72d, he told me enthusiastically, was "the largest field artillery brigade in the free world." As it happened, Colonel Kelly had been bus monitor that very morning. Still the diffident guest, I did not mention I thought little of this exercise in military democracy. If the balloon ever did go up in Europe, and Colonel Kelly was on the Wurzburg run when it happened, I could imagine the congressional investigating committee: "And you, Colonel Kelly, were where? On a school bus? As bus monitor?" A real career breaker, that.

Democratization had also recast the officers' club. It was now called the Community Center and membership was available to senior noncoms as well as officers; the dining room in fact was open to all personnel on post, including civilians and German nationals; only the bar and the game room were exclusively reserved for club members. I had lunch at the center with the brigade commander, a bird colonel in his early forties, twenty-two years in the army, with a broad open face that made him seem larger than he actually was. By my calculations, he would have been twelve when I rotated back to the States, yet I had the uncomfortable feeling throughout the meal that he was about to call me "son," in that way colonels in the movies always calm frightened privates just before combat: "Only a fool's not afraid at a moment like this, son." "You too, sir?" "Me too, son."

We talked about community relations, a subject I suspect bored him no less than it bored me, but a safe topic to take up with a civilian. The colonel said the post was represented at the Fasching festival in town every year and that he expected some three hundred Germans from town to attend a reception at his house on post the day before the Fourth of July. Even alerts, he said, were now synchronized with German authorities to avoid traffic tie-ups on the autobahns. I asked if the Russians could be expected to attack at times of light traffic, a question he did not choose to answer. He asked how relations had been between the post and the town in my day. I said the only time we ever saw any Germans on post was when a mother came up to complain to the battery commander that a GI had knocked up her daughter. He smiled. "Some things," he said, "never change."

Then it was time to go. The colonel gave me a set of bar glasses printed with the artillery's red crossed-cannon logo and a baseball hat that said, "Re-Up 72d FA." Not likely. I did not expect to pass that way again. Thomas Wolfe was right.

XV

"I WONDER if an army could survive without whores," I had written in my notebook before leaving New York. Sociology on the cheap, a way to justify my revisiting the red-light district in Frankfurt. Not for any prurient reason, of course (of course!), but in the interests of research, one more stop on this middle-aged journey of discovery. Thirty years later, the red-light district was still in the same location, frozen in time, a compass reading I had never lost, two square blocks across from the *hauptbahnhof*, bisected by the Kaiserstrasse. Off-duty American servicemen prowled in packs, whites with whites, blacks with blacks, easily recognizable in their shorts and T-shirts and Air Jordan sneakers, music blaring from their boogie blasters, an aural blitz defining both their space and their attitude toward those that they, from the arsenal of democracy, were pledged to defend. In the long spring twilight, a few whores were already working the streets, more upmarket than I remembered, with Hermès scarves and Vuitton bags and Fiorucci T-shirts. Several were Asian, German-speaking, a few black, also German-speaking, I suspect daughters left behind when an earlier generation of GIs had ZIed. The potential john was unmistakable, a male tourist pretending to window-shop, waiting for the whore to catch up; then the whispered conversation, no sale, with the tourist continuing his stroll until accosted once more, that classic looker, the talker who got off by negotiating.

It was the same, but also subtly different, a nighttown of the loony that had undergone, in the three decades since I had last been there, a kind of retail sexual gentrification. The paraphernalia of tumescence had eclipsed sex as the area's primary business, with surrogate gratification more important, in a mercantile sense, than gratification itself. There were sex shops and sex *kines* and sex bars and sex supermarkets, and in every window, decals of the credit cards and bank traveler's checks accepted—Mitsui Bank of Japan, Bank Leumi of Israel, Banca Popolare di Milano, Algemene Bank Nederland, Bank Bumiputra Malaysia Berhad, Banco do Brasil, Hongkong & Shanghai Banking Corporation, Oesterreichische Laenderbank, United Bank of Kuwait, only Antarctica and the Arctic of the world's seven continents unrepresented.

Here was Wendell Willkie's one world, a true entrepôt of the horny. The sex supermarkets were like K Marts dedicated to lubricity, with baskets and shopping carts for the volume buyer. Tour buses disgorged visitors from Oslo and Ostend, Seoul and Singapore. The furtive behavior, the lust for anonymity that I had always associated with the commercial sexual ramble, was passé, aggressive comparison shopping the norm. Notebook in hand, product specificity my aim, the avid researcher (as I still insisted I was) shopped in the largest of the twenty-four-hour markets, three stories of sex aids, bowing to small Japanese, elbowing aside burly Norsemen. It was June, but the crowds, mostly men, plus a few women hefting vibrators as if they were fresh bananas, behaved as if there were only three shopping days remaining until Christmas, fighting over the limited supply of the newest, most up-to-date dildo as if it were that season's equivalent of the Cabbage Patch Doll. The ethic was that of the dollar-day sale. What I missed was the sense of sin, the hint of danger, that had always made sex for hire so stimulating to the young lapsed Catholic I had once been. It was a stimulus augmented by the daydream of spelling out every sordid detail in confession, Bless me, Father, for I have sinned, as if my fervidly imagined rendering of how the heights of Aphrodite were scaled and conquered could tempt the celibate priest from God's path.

I had always thought I had a feel for the aberrant, but the sheer variety of the hardware and software on the three floors made me consider the possibility that I had led a more sheltered life than I cared to admit. Every counter contained a revelation in blue. There were Fat Mama videos, featuring grotesquely fat women performing the unmentionable to the rhythms of the Swedish rock group Abba. Twin dildos with a single power source so that two lesbians could do each other simultaneously. There were erection supports and penis rings and penis pumps and ribbed designer condoms so elaborate they came with instruction sheets, and made the French ticklers of my army days seem uninspired. And richly veined plastic cocks that fit over the real thing in the event of impotence or excessive use. On a shelf, small bottles of Spanish Fly (*Spanische Fliege*), a whole row arranged like spices in a rack, one brand engagingly reinforced with vitamin E. In the Catholic schoolyards of my adolescence, we had endlessly argued the existence not of God but of Spanish fly, and whether too much would drive you insane, and whether the risk was worth it, yes, oh, yes, what a way to die, even without vitamin E added.

The place could have used a floorwalker ("Mezzanine—lubricants and aphrodisiacs"). There were creams and lotions with names like Gay Kum and Pussy Glide, each claiming to prolong intercourse and enhance orgasm. There were magazines for pedophiles and magazines that specialized in fellatio and others in anal intercourse, as well as every conceivable kind of gay congress; it was as if AIDS had not intruded on the market sensibility. There was a pornographic dinner service—four pornographic plates and four pornographic napkins laid out on a pornographic tablecloth of a couple sixty-nining. The most intriguing items were inflatable female dolls that could be blown up life-size with a bicycle pump, a race for every taste—China Girl (with short black bangs) and African Queen (curly Afro, and no sexual ambivalence in spite of the name's androgynous implication) and California Sweet (long Malibu blonde). Fully inflated, each doll had tits and nipples and buns that jiggled and plastic pubic hair, both the mouth and the vagina perfectly O-shaped, with a small vibrator behind each O. The user could penetrate the orifice of his choice, and be fellated or fucked by the vibrator attached. It was more innocent in my day. You picked up a whore, you got laid, then you wondered what you would do with the rest of your life. Now you could get sucked and fucked by a life-size doll, five foot two, eyes of blue. Age would not wither nor gravity exert its will, no emotional commitment and no chance of a social disease. There was also the advantage of not having to meet the doll's landlord and his nuclear family sitting around the radio in the next room. Still: getting blown by California Sweet seemed a prelude to suicide.

I STOPPED for a beer in an all-night video arcade. There was a live peep show in the back, seventeen cubicles enclosing a circular stage. Each cubicle had a window, a screen and a coin meter. When a coin was inserted, the screen went up, and through the small window the viewer could watch a naked woman dance to a nondescript rock beat for as long as he paid, one deutsche mark per minute, five marks five minutes, the screen slamming down when time was up. Faces vacant, hips and bums moving to no apparent rhythmic scheme, the dancers played to the shadowy faces in the windows, occasionally finger-fucking or, in a spasm of hostility, pressing a crotch up against the glass. They changed in midset, a black dancer replaced by a white, who in time was replaced by a Eurasian with no pubic hair, each modestly pulling on a robe before she disappeared offstage.

In the front of the arcade, by the bar, there were dozens of video games, most predicated on the hallucinatory notion of Rambo rampant—games with names like Street Fighter, Rampage, Italy 1943, Gauntlet III and Rolling Thunder, not the Bob Dylan tour but the search-and-destroy fiasco of the Vietnam War, now metamorphosed into a video triumph, revisionist history for the functionally illiterate. The dancers from the peep show kibitzed as they waited for their next set, or a trick, whichever came first. One—the Eurasian—was pumping coins into a game called Contra. She was wearing a red Marine Corps T-shirt with the recruiting slogan "We Need a Few Good Men," which seemed not entirely inappropriate to her calling. As part of my protective coloring, I was wearing my "Re-Up 72d FA" cap, which she plucked from my head and put on hers. "You a master sergeant?" she asked.

I was somewhat nonplussed. "Why do you think that?"

"You too old to be a private. You got to be plenty big fuckup to still be a private."

She asked if I wanted to play Contra. I inserted some coins

and concentrated on the video screen. The game appeared to be about a jungle war, with two freedom-loving contra mercenaries taking on a totalitarian army that had subverted a southern democracy. A player could make the two contras ford rivers and somersault over the enemy, and with their outsized automatic weapons they were more than a match for the numerically superior subversives. With bandannas wrapped around their heads, the two contras were handsome specimens, their names not José or Juan or Comandante Suicido but Lance and Bill, an incongruity I was indelicate enough to mention.

"What the fuck you talking about anyway, Sarge?"

I let her keep my cap and wandered back onto the Kaiserstrasse. Outside a twenty-four-hour sex *Kine*, a born-again American Christian was doing God's work. He was wearing khaki slacks and white sneakers and a windbreaker on which was written, "A Christian Ministry—Myron." Myron was middle-aged, well-groomed, with graying hair. "The Lord is my shepherd," Myron intoned, an open Bible in his hand. "And how many of you, like sheep, have gone astray?" Myron knew his audience; this was a whole flock of lost sheep, mostly whores and their would-be tricks. His remarks were translated into German by an overweight woman with a microphone, Mary Magdalene to Myron's savior. "You can be new creatures," Myron said. "How would you like to be born again?" A drunk heckled from the edge of the crowd. Myron waited patiently for the translation and then invoked Nicodemus. "Do you not think it's possible to enter your mother's womb and be born again?" His voice rose. "I say to you, God has a plan."

Myron's acolytes, young, a few black, all carrying Bibles, worked the crowd. I trailed one of his female ministers as she and her translator tried to tell a prostitute of God's plan. "Tell her," the minister said, "how much her life will be improved if she abandons carnality and allows herself to be born again." I think God's surrogate would have had more luck with California Sweet.

On the fringes of the crowd, I suddenly spotted what I thought a familiar face. A youngish English historian and cold warrior, a specialist in Middle Europe. A few years before, we had spent an afternoon together arguing in a Gloucestershire garden. We were both pissed. His name was H. and he had a wife, a girlfriend, a boyfriend, a taste for the high life, and strong right-wing Tory views. The argument was about the fight at Oxford over whether the university should award an honorary doctorate to Margaret Thatcher. Many of the lefty dons thought not, because of the Thatcher cuts in the education budget and because of a general distaste for her policies. The right-wingers, including my companion, both agreed with her budget cuts and thought that, more important, it did no good to insult a sitting prime minister. I said I would have voted against awarding Thatcher the honorary degree. It had nothing to do with her policies. I just felt that a great university should only give a politician the contempt he or she deserved. We then had segued into a discussion of the Vietnam War. H. thought it was a worthy endeavor for all the reasons those who thought it worthy usually advanced—a great power had to honor its commitments, the need to check communism, the need not to appear ineffectual in the eyes of the world. I told him I thought he was full of shit, a level of demotic discourse at which I am more comfortable. H. took this with reasonably good grace. "Mind you," he said, "I didn't have to fight in it." "And mind you," I replied, "you wouldn't have."

So here we both were. In the Frankfurt red-light district, the last place in the world where either one of us would ever have expected to meet the other again. Maybe he was researching too. Was it really he? Is there such a thing as an exact double, that staple of detective fiction? Our eyes locked. I hoped my face did not show the look of panic I thought I saw on his. Fuck it. Brazen it out. "Hello," I said. "Haven't seen you since that weekend at Fiona's."

"*Bitte?*"

My confidence wavered. "We had smoked trout by the brook. I said you were full of shit."

A blizzard of German. He was looking for an escape. One of Myron's ministers blocked his way. "Have you heard the parable of the lost sheep?"

"Bugger off." In English.

Ahh. "Give my best to Fiona."

INTERNAL AFFAIRS INVESTIGATION (*cont'd*):

Q: Was it really H.?
A: I thought it was. Later I was told he was in Poland that month.
Q: You didn't like him when you met him?
A: I thought he was a pontificating horse's ass.
Q: Was this your way of showing he was a horse's ass?
A: Perhaps.
Q: Isn't that mean-spirited?
A: I never said the harps weren't mean-spirited. Especially about the Brits. Beating up on the Brits is one of the more pleasant aspects of being a harp.
Q: Is this whole thing a game? Were you in fact fucking around? Is your clinical interest in the subject just a

beard? So that no one would think you were fucking around? Did you in fact buy condoms, sex aids, French ticklers, *Spanische Fliege*, the works?

A: Perhaps.

Q: How much of what you are telling is true?

A: Let me tell you a story. A few years before Lillian Hellman died, my wife and I had dinner with her one night in Los Angeles. She was spending the winter in Mary Tyler Moore's house in Bel Air, a big job, with round-the-clock help. As Lillian got older, with her chronic emphysema, she couldn't take the New York winters anymore, and either she would rent a house in L.A. or someone would lend her one. We saw a lot of her in these years. She had just published her book *Maybe*, the third volume in the trilogy that began with *An Unfinished Woman* and *Pentimento*. Now she had taken a lot of static about the earlier two, especially the part in *Pentimento* that became the movie *Julia*. The books were supposedly autobiographical, but there were charges around that she had fiddled with the truth. I thought the charges were beside the point, because she was after all a storyteller, and a storyteller tells stories. Anyway, at dinner that night I told her I liked *Maybe*, which I did. What I didn't tell her was that I liked it a hell of a lot better than either *An Unfinished Woman* or *Pentimento*. Telling her that would have been an invitation to getting my head chopped off, because she was a mean, ornery number until the day she died. And she said the most interesting thing. She said she could have saved herself a whole lot of grief had she published *Maybe* before the other two, *Maybe* with its oh-so-tentative title invoking the possibility of nuances beyond the facts, that in the failure of memory, this is how she chose to remember. If *Maybe* had come first, she might have been spared the shit she had to take for reinventing her life. What she was saying was that her life was for her to interpret as she saw fit, and fuck-all to anyone who said she couldn't. The pattern would have been set with the word "Maybe."

Q: Is that what you claim you've been doing?

A: Maybe.

Q: And now to Ireland?

A: Yes.

Q: Were you happy about going there finally?

A: Not particularly.

XVI

In fact, I had always resisted the idea of Ireland, whence Poppa had set out in 1869, at the age of twelve, to make his way in the New World. And make it he had, although perhaps with results, two generations later with me, that he might not have imagined, and would certainly not have appreciated. I was not deeply stirred by the Troubles, I had no allegiance to the IRA, nor even any particular enthusiasm for Yeats or O'Casey; St. Patrick's Day meant only a parade that hopelessly gridlocked midtown Manhattan. There were four different stages of the Irish-American experience—immigrant, outcast, assimilated, deracinated. I was in stage four, deracinated in the sense that I never thought my Irish background had anything to do with a place called Ireland. My being Irish was more a component of a parochial school education, of nuns and priests with a flair for discipline and a taste for corporal punishment. The result was that I thought of Ireland, when I thought of it at all, less as a place on the map than as a sentimental fantasy land where geriatric curates with false and hearty brogues chaperoned the annual parish pilgrimage of the Altar Society and the Aquinas Club and the Sodality of

Mary, widows and maiden ladies who stocked up on Belleek saucers and Waterford crystal and linen cocktail napkins appliquéd with shamrocks, the perfect wedding present for Moira Kinsella when she married Fainting Phil Hickey's boy, Dennis, him with the walleye and the grand future with Wally Mahoney over in the Department of Weights and Measures there.

And yet here I was, on my way to Ireland for the first time. There is nothing like a disagreeable experience with one's health to make one curious about something one has never been curious about before. As the airbus from Frankfurt to Dublin dropped out of the clouds, I stared out the window for a first look. The Irish Sea was slate gray, the dark brooding landscape below swept with rain. In a country of so many soothing hues of green, I wondered why Aer Lingus painted its jets with one the color of bile. I searched the newspaper given me by the flight attendant for clues as to what to expect. The *Irish Times* was full of tales of sodomy. "Dublin Man Jailled for Buggery of Student, 17," ran a headline on page 8, and deeper in the paper there was another, one-sentence story: "LtCdr Peter Harrison, 43, who is at the center of an inquiry into alleged indecent assaults aboard his ship, the destroyer Nottingham, has been flown home from the South Atlantic and assigned to a desk job." The new Ireland, I thought, the country where Joyce and O'Casey had trouble being published. Now buggery was all the rage in the respectable press.

In the holding pattern, the mind began to play. The saga of Student, 17, was a conventional cautionary tale of life in the city (a chat about film outside a cinema, a pint in a pub "and a mineral for the youth," and then oral sex and "buggering . . . on waste ground off Adelaide Road," finally a trial and the standard psychiatric defense: "O'Shea [the buggerer] . . . could not complete the sexual act and this led to frustration and aggression . . ."). The lieutenant commander, however, was another story. Here was the only kind of military history that really interested me; I was reminded of those parenthetical asides in Samuel Eliot Morison's history of the U.S. Navy in World War II, the ellipses about the captain who committed suicide aboard ship, or the officer relieved of his command: why did the suicide do it? where was the relieved officer assigned next? I tried to imagine the lieutenant commander's flight back to England, his first morning at his new posting. "Good morning, yeoman." "Good morning, sir." Not a hint of a smirk, but the word in the petty officers' mess was keep your bum puckered.

On the ground, the rain slanted in sheets. "It was a glorious morning," my cabbie assured me when I cleared customs, in the way of hack drivers the world over, spinning a tale that the arriving traveler had just missed the most glorious Wednesday morning in June since Eamon De Valera was a virgin. He could scarcely contain his excitement that I had just come from Germany. He was off there the following weekend, a football tour with the Irish national soccer team, participants for the first time in the European championships, less a fan's odyssey than an eight-day pissup in Darmstadt, Stuttgart, and Frankfurt. He was especially looking forward to the Sunday match with England in Stuttgart. "Their lads won't pull anything on us," he said. He meant not the English team, but the hooligan English football fans, the Visigoths of the eighties, who had sacked cities and stadiums across the Continent; their arrival meant police alerts and a search of videotapes for familiar faces from earlier riots. I had the sense the cabbie was anticipating a fine brawl, that psychically he had already fit a roll of coins in his fist, the better to smash an English face; there was nothing half so satisfying as an old score settled, a contemporary reckoning of the Easter Rising.

Dublin west of the Liffey, the river that bisects the city, fashionable on its eastern shore, mean and blotchy on its western, reminded me of the Frog Hollow of my youth. Kelly and Modeen, read the names on the too garish storefronts; Sheridan and O'Shea. Even the omnipresent video stores did not relieve the primal gloom of economic deprivation, of piss-elegant Georgian houses turned into blighted, rotting tenements. My spirits only began to lift when I saw a panel truck stuck in traffic on the O'Connell Street Bridge, on its side the slogan "If Dunne Can't Do It, It Can't Be Dunne." A rule to live by. It was Dublin's millennium, 888 to 1988, and the city was making an effort to spruce itself up. "Happy Birthday, Dublin," read the sign on the back of the bus, "From Action Drains, Ltd." Outside Leinster House, the seat of Ireland's government, where the Dail (the 148-member Chamber of Deputies) and the Seanad (the 60-member Senate) sit, there was a demonstration, farmers protesting a tax increase. They were all neatly dressed, ties and jackets, and they carried banners decrying the tax increase. Suddenly a gust of wind raised the hairpiece of one of the farmers, and to the great glee of the protesters the wig bounced across Kildale Street as if it were a piece of Dynel tumbleweed.

Everywhere there were platoons of miniskirts and punk haircuts window-shopping, as if on slow drill. Ireland was a country where nearly half the population of four million was under twenty-five. Where once ninety-five percent of the people attended Sunday mass, church attendance had dropped to an all-time low of eighty-seven percent, a scandal in the eyes of the clergy, still rote religion to a skeptic like myself. The young belonged to a culture more attuned to MTV and Bob Geldof than to novenas, First Fridays, Holy Days of Obligation and making their Easter duty. Intuitively I had the sense that those young window-shoppers on Nassau Street paid scant attention to the catechism lessons they had been taught by the good nuns at Our Lady of Sorrows. Any doubts I might have had were almost immediately dispelled by a mini with purple-tinted albino hair who caught me staring from the window of my taxi. "Take a good look," she yelled from outside a record shop. "You won't see tits like this again in your lifetime." A gift of repartee I would wager she had not learned at the knee of Sister Theodosius.

So HERE I AM, sitting in the lounge at the Shelbourne on St. Stephen's Green, it's nearly 11 P.M., still light outside, and I am half or even three-quarters pissed, two whiskeys before dinner, a half-bottle of Côtes-du-Rhône, and when that was killed, a glass of vin rouge and then a beer and after that a vintage port, altogether quite a package. All this downed while having dinner alone in a French restaurant off Lower Baggott Street. Good value at the other tables. To my left four American businessmen trying to hustle a local in pharmaceuticals. Three of the Americans were youngish, gray in demeanor and attire, shoes with laces, pants with cuffs; the fourth was the talker and the killer: side vents, bright shirt, cuff links, no pleasantries, your problem, as we see it—heavy nodding from his three pals—is the generalized economic slump, the depressed conditions re manpower and a tax situation that is not, all things considered, as advantageous as we—my associates and I—would prefer for an investment opportunity.

The local in pharmaceuticals pressed on gamely, invoking the 1990s, a decade of promise, Ireland rising like the phoenix. . . . It's those ashes that concern me, side vents murmured, not one to be taken in by a fancy allusion. The local caved: What do you want from me then? One of the gray suits spoke for the first time: More concessions.

Equal value at the table for eight across from mine. Three American tourist couples entertaining a Dublin couple. The three American wives, dressed to the hilt, immediately sat next to each other, and when one of the husbands suggested a "boy, girl, boy, girl" seating arrangement, a wife said, "Oh, you wouldn't be interested in our girl talk," a plan that effectively froze the Irish wife from their conversation. She sat at the far end of the table, two men on either side of her, one her husband, the other the oldest of the American men, who talked nonstop about his navy experiences, which seemed to consist of getting to know San Diego. "That California," he kept on saying, "is something else." The Dublin wife stared into space, drumming on the table with breadstick.

Back to the Shelbourne for a nightcap in the lounge, one too many; I had to hold one eyelid shut so I could keep the room in focus. I was suddenly overcome by how much, after twenty-five years of cohabitation and marriage, I hated to travel alone. I long for the idea, with its promise of extracurricular rambles, but I hate the actuality. I am not, after all, the seeker after romance that I fancy myself as being, but only a seeker after an adapter to plug into my computer so I can type my notes; the German plug will not work nor the French; I need an Irish plug. I calculated the time, wondering if I should call my wife, who was still in California; our telephone bills, when we are separated, both on the road, are enormous. Eight hours' time difference; when I get up in the morning, she will just be getting home from dinner with the gay movie producer; when I go out to dinner, she will be getting ready for lunch with the political candidate's speechwriter and campaign adviser. Finally I call Los Angeles from the lounge; I don't wish I was there, I just wish I was not getting drunk alone here. He's a fucking snake, I warn her unnecessarily about the speechwriter when the call is finally put through. She already knows it, but this is the kind of advice we pass on to each other after twenty-five years. Be wary: wariness, we both believe, is the greatest of virtues; if you know the downside, you are rarely surprised; better a redundant warning about a snake than no warning at all. Information is always useful: It won't come up, but don't forget that the campaign adviser's first wife went down in that American crash in Chicago in '78. It was something else she already knew, as I knew she would: redundancy redux. She read me excerpts from a magazine piece by someone we both knew and detested, this at a cost of God knows how many dollars per minute. "An artful presentation of a coherent untruth," she says. "Now I know what Mary McCarthy meant about Lillian Hellman."

"Not bad," I said.

"How's it going?"

"What the fuck am I doing here?"

MY PLAN was to get an Irish passport, to which I was entitled because Poppa had been born in Ireland. The application forms from the Foreign Ministry were forwarded to me by the Irish Information Office in New York, and were no more complicated than the instructions of any other bureaucracy. Under what amounts to an Irish law of return, the child or grandchild of someone of Irish birth or citizenship is eligible for "nationality" in the Republic of Ireland without forfeiting citizenship in the country of his primary allegiance; nationality confers on the recipient all the benefits of citizenship except the franchise. Since my mother—Poppa's daughter—was the parent through whom I could claim an Irish passport, I would need a copy of both her birth and her marriage certificates, each in the "vault form," that is, with the birthplace of her father listed, and a copy of my own birth certificate, also in the vault form, in my case with my mother's birthplace listed. These were easily secured in Hartford. With them in hand, I could then try to secure a copy of my grandfather's birth records. Poppa was born in 1857, and as no civil records were kept in Ireland until 1864, I would need his baptismal record to certify his Irish birth. For this I would have to apply directly to the parish where he had been christened. His obituaries, the only verification I had, listed his birthplace as Strokestown, in County Roscommon, and his parents as William and Mary Burns; he was, according to the *Catholic Transcript*, one of eighteen children, six belonging to his stepmother, the rest the issue of his father's two marriages. Again I called the Irish Information Office, which in time sent me the appropriate pages in the annual *Irish Catholic Directory* listing the parishes in the county. Either I could write for his baptismal certificate or I could visit the parish in Strokestown in person. Once I had a certified copy of Poppa's baptismal record, I could then present all the documentation to the Foreign Office in Dublin and apply for my Irish passport.

I told myself I wanted the passport because I usually visited Europe every year, and it would make travel easier. Ireland was a member of the European Economic Community—the Common Market—and the lines for EEC passport holders were invariably shorter at Common Market ports of entry, the customs inspections cursory. With an Irish passport, I would also not need a visa for France, which after the 1986 terrorist bombings in Paris began requiring one for travelers from non-member nations. There was another terrorism factor; in the event of a skyjacking, it would perhaps be more propitious to be carrying an Irish rather than an American passport. All this rationalization was of course nonsense. My wife would still need a French visa, and if during a skyjacking I presented an Irish and she an American passport, I suspect, in the event we both survived, that there would be a terminal strain on the marriage. The fact is I wanted an Irish passport for the simple reason that I was eligible for one. Trying to get one would both add structure to my journey and force me into that examination of my Irish background that I had always so rigorously rejected.

REJECTED BECAUSE I hated the history. It was the Famine, of course, the failure of the potato crop in successive years between 1845 and 1847, that triggered the largest emigration of the Irish to America, those very Irish I and so many like me spend so much time trying to trace. A million and a half people died of the Great Hunger and its concomitant fevers, and another million left Ireland, most ultimately to America, most never to return, most with the sketchiest of histories:

> *With a bundle on my shoulder*
> *Sure there's no man could be bolder*
> *I'm leaving dear old Ireland without warning.*
> *For I've lately took the notion*
> *To cross the briny ocean*
> *I'm bound for Philadelphia in the morning.*

And to Boston, New York, and Hartford. Who went? What was the trip like? There are scant clues in the emigration logs. Almost no records were kept at such major ports of embarkation as Galway, Derry, Dublin, Belfast and Queenstown. Further evidence vanished when the Public Record Office in Dublin was consumed by fire in 1922, and earlier, in 1910, when the British Board of Trade destroyed Cunard Line passenger records dating back to 1840; it was as if the Board of Trade wanted to erase the history of those dark years, when every packet across the Atlantic, every steerage passenger, was a rebuke to the mean spirit of Ireland's conqueror.

Records, however, are easier to erase than memories, and it is from memories that the Irish oral tradition is drawn. It was a miserable trip, fifty to eighty days depending on the weather, steerage for a family of eight costing, in 1855, twenty-four pounds, food and water included, with bedding and eating utensils provided by the passenger. Sometimes whole parishes abandoned Ireland together, as when Father Thomas Hore, a parish priest in County Wexford, sailed from Liverpool in November 1850 on the ship *Ticonderoga*, bound for New Orleans with 462 members of his congregation. The bare facts of a given passenger list often concealed a larger story. "Laborer . . . servant . . . farmer" were the job occupations entered after the names of the passengers on the ship *James*, out of Newry on May 10, 1849, destination New York. The frequency with which passengers listed themselves as menials, however, was often just a way around a British policy forbidding the emigration of the skilled labor necessary to power England's industrial revolution.

Laborer, servant, farmer, spinster, child, infant: what was their past and where to begin looking? For the poor Irish—that is, the majority—in those harsh and often bloody centuries, the keeping of records was hardly a priority, and prey, as one book delicately put it, "to historical circumstances"— in other words, a subject peasant class and a Catholic clergy sometimes scarcely more literate than the members of their flock. Baptisms often entailed a sixpence offering to the church, no small sum in families of a dozen children or more with crippling rents to be paid to absentee landlords; better to save the sixpence and pour a little water from the well or the creek over the head of the wee one, who in all likelihood would not survive the winter anyway, so no harm done the baby not being on the parish rolls. Pious the poor Irish may have been, but as the proverb in Poppa's scrapbook said, "The priest's pig gets most of the porridge."

In the Genealogy Bookshop, on Nassau Street, I picked up *Handbook on Irish Genealogy*, a trove of hints on where to go, what to look for, and how to proceed. Right off I learned that the time-honored Irish custom was to name the firstborn son after the paternal grandfather, the second after the maternal; the two oldest daughters were similarly named after their grandmothers. (Among my siblings, only the maternal grandparents were so honored; my own daughter is named Quintana Roo, after the state in Mexico, a Christian name, I would suspect, not much in vogue in rural Ireland.) Because many parish registers and burial records prior to the mid-nineteenth century no longer exist, if indeed they were ever kept at all, gravestone inscriptions are often the only means of tracing earlier generations. Here the ancestor hunter can call upon the Association for the Preservation of the Memorials of the Dead, which publishes a journal containing thousands of inscriptions gathered from stones all over Ireland. A complete set of the journals, now running to a dozen volumes, can be found in the library of the Genealogical

Office, on Kildare Street in Dublin. The inscriptions, if nothing else, often make good reading, as this one taken from a stone in County Fermanagh:

To the
Memory
Denis McCabe
Fidler
Who fell out of the
St. Patrick's Barge Belong
ing to Sr
James Caldwell, Bart

Beware ye fidlers of ye
Fidler's fate
Nor tempt ye deep least ye
repent too late
You ever have been deem'd to
Foes
then shun ye lake till with whisk'y flows
on firm land only Exercise your skill
there you may play and drink yr fill

For those whose ancestors were either relatively affluent or affiliated with the Established (or Protestant) Church of Ireland, there would be official records, and any serious search must begin at the Public Record Office in Dublin's Four Courts Building, on Inn's Quay. Poppa, of course, was neither well off (no fancy expensive burial monuments for the Burnses) nor Established Church, but the Public Record Office was a browser's paradise. Of particular interest were the documents from the years before 1864, when the keeping of civic records became for the first time a public trust. There were valuation and tax records, tithe books, census records,

diocesan wills, collections of family papers, genealogical ab-
stracts compiled from prerogative wills, and Church of Ireland
parish records; nearly a thousand of these parish registers, half
the total, originally consigned there for safekeeping by the
Master of Rolls, were destroyed in that 1922 fire at the Public
Record Office. In the titles of the more historically piquant
miscellaneous records was an inkling of what life must have
been like in this most depressed and contentious of England's
satrapies: Registry of Popish Clergy, Diocese of Meath, 1782–
83; Registry of Cholera Cases, 1832; Deserted Children's Account Book, 1842–64.

For the grandson of Dominick Francis Burns, nothing in
the public record applied: N/A. It was on to Strokestown,
County Roscommon, and the parish register, now incorpo-
rating, according to the *Catholic Directory*, the ancient parishes of Bumblin, Kiltrustan, Cloonfinlough and Lissunuffy.
That is, if William Burns, married twice, father and stepfather
of eighteen, had, that summer of 1857, the extra sixpence to
spare. I wondered about the fate of those other seventeen;
family memory on this score was faulty, perhaps even inten-
tionally so. In Hartford, we were the family on the hill, micks
of privilege; as if to the manor born, we did not like to think
of those who had stayed behind, and their offspring's offspring,
and their offspring, those Burns cousins I would perhaps finally
get a chance to meet. If they were there, would I come forward? Or hide behind the Dunne and observe, the writer's
trick? If Dunne Can't Do It, It Can't Be Dunne. A deep
slogan, that, deeper than I thought.

WEST ON THE N4, Dublin's sprawl soon ending, and then, in
Meath, the Irish countryside, and green, green as far as the

eye could see: sage, olive and beryl; jade, emerald and mala-
chite; celadon, reseda and Nile; grass, moss and turf; pea
green, sea green, bottle green: green. Flocks of sheep dotted
the hillsides, different flocks marked with different Day-Glo
colors for identification, blue and orange and heliotrope and
chartreuse, the dyes over head and shoulders giving the sheep
the look of failed punk rockers. On the highway, there were
occasional discreet warnings by the side of the road, nearly
always obscured by the hedgerow: just simple white signs,
each with a black circle in the middle, and the words "Danger—Accident—Black Spot"; every black spot marked the
site of a fatal automobile accident. At an L-shaped curve on
a narrow winding road off the main highway, I pulled over to
examine one of the signs. Just beyond the black spot was a
stone marker, topped with a cross: "Kate Forde—Miltown,
Galway—Accidentally Killed 12 May 1976—Aged 19 Years."

Roscommon lies smack in the middle of the country. Irish
schoolchildren are taught that the landscape of the Midlands,
running south from County Roscommon through Longford,
Westmeath, Offaly and Laois, is like the flat base of a tea
saucer, the raised rim representing the mountains surrounding
at every point of the compass. A mundane image, made more
so by the corollary always appended: tea is usually spilled, and
the slosh in the saucer's bottom is what the Midlands' ground-
scape and weather are like—wet. In bog and meadow, water
seems to give way to water—rivers, lakes, streams, canals,
ditches, gullies, backwaters; from the air, the landscape seems
like an archipelago of soggy islands. "A vast Serbonian bog,"
the nineteenth-century Irish novelist Maria Edgeworth called
it. She was one of twenty-one children by her father's four
wives, so short—four feet seven—that she was strung up and
hung when young in a vain attempt to stretch her to greater

height. This part of Ireland was not to her taste. "Aptly called," she wrote, " 'the yellow dwarf's country.' "

It was my kind of place, this yellow dwarf's country. "Nuns and midgets," I had once, no: twice, perhaps thrice, written, "that's the ticket." It is as close as I have ever come to an aesthetic. In travel, I dislike sightseeing. I avoid churches, shrines, holy places, great houses, tombs, museums and grottoes. I tolerate battlefields and battlements only if they have some historical relevance to the century in which I live—the Normandy beaches, say, or Anzio, or Château-Thierry. Venice leaves me cold. "The rationalist mind has always had its doubts about Venice," Mary McCarthy wrote in *Venice Observed*; I must have a rationalist's mind. Guides and guidebooks fill me with dismay and consternation; "famous in early Christian days" is a phrase that induces a torpor and a lust to move on. I want to drive, walk, come upon things by accident or because I'm lost, not have them pointed out, a provenance explained, in the middle of a tour. I had been visiting Paris every year for ten years before I finally managed to hit the Louvre, and then only while looking for cover from a sudden cloudburst. How much better to come upon the Mona Lisa that way. I had even seen the sewers of Paris and the Canal St. Martin and the slums of Belleville and Ménilmontant before I saw the sublime stained-glass windows of La Sainte-Chapelle; and was more likely to spend a Sunday with the newspapers in the Parc des Buttes-Chaumont in the industrial 19th arrondissement than in the Jardins des Tuileries. So: nuns and midgets and now yellow dwarfs: ahh.

I crossed the Shannon, Ireland's Amazon, into Roscommon. Ros—a gently wooded height; Coman—the first bishop of the see: hence Roscommon. It was after nine, an evening in mid-June, and the countryside was still bathed in that won-

drous lambent light so mysterious and glorious to someone
from the subtropics, where the darkness arrives like a thief,
darting through the sky, a sprinter on steroids. I had booked
a room at the Abbey Hotel, in Roscommon town, formerly a
Catholic abbey, as its name suggested, although the young
woman at the desk did not know when or for what order and
seemed to take it amiss that I was interested enough to ask.
I was just wondering, I said, only continuing the conversation
because I had no one else to talk to, how many hotels in rural
Ireland had once been God's dormitories. She looked at me
blankly, her face lobster pink from that day's sun, a cluster
of sunburn blisters running down her bare arms. Fair mick
skin, like mine, so sensitive a night light could raise a blister;
only a nun in full habit—cowl, wimple and veil—should venture out in the summer's glare. Harp genes, a subject for a
later dissertation. Not, however, with her. I had the feeling
that she was just itching to ask, What the fook are you babbling about?

After dinner, I went for a walk. It was past ten o'clock, but
the sun still hung high in the sky to the west, toward Mayo
and the Atlantic, a perfect orange orb throwing the three-
quarter light of early dusk, so eerie at this time of night. Outside a pub I could hear the sound of amplified music. There
was a van parked at the curb, and written on the side of the
van the words "Baritone Dan, the Street Singing Man." Inside, Baritone Dan and pub regulars were serenading the bar-
tender, a young man whose stomach spilled over his belt and
who was getting married the following weekend. I sat next
to an elderly drunk who knew half the lyrics of all the songs,
and the words he did not know he filled in with "Dum de
dum dum, she was nineteen and a bride to be, dum de dum
dum," all the while beating his hand on the bar in a misguided

idea of rhythm. Suddenly he fixed me in his gaze. "Ask me my favorite drink," he demanded. I asked him his favorite drink. "The next one," he roared. I knew I had been had, and set him up, and Baritone Dan as well.

I returned to the hotel before eleven. The sun was like the drunk in the pub, not wanting to call it a day. In the parlor, attended by a barman, I watched a BBC television documentary about the IRA, the Provos, and the continuing war in the North. The show had the reassuring familiarity of cliché. An arms shipment seized at a roundabout. The magic word Kalashnikov. The announcer: "The massive shipment of arms will be used to fight what the Provos call 'the long war.'" A roadblock; a computer check of a license plate: "This car is a 1979 Fiat Spyder, silver, registered to Brid Sheehan, Castlereagh." An endless funeral, innocent victims, families weeping at the cemetery grave site, the announcer intoning, as I knew he would, "And then they said the rosary." Lastly onscreen a plummy English MP with an overview, a silk handkerchief spilling out of his breast pocket: "I want to have an absolutely clear conscience about this. . . ." The barman, who had not appeared to be watching, suddenly said, more to himself than to me, "The fook has a taste for luxuries." It was a voice I instantly recognized; it had the unmistakably belligerent cadences of parochial school.

About Roscommon, county and town, the guidebooks have embarrassingly little to say; it is as if the yellow dwarfs were still casting their spell. In the greensward just north of the town stand the ruins of the obligatory Norman castle: another prop. Then there is the Sacred Heart Church, on a rise dominating the entire area, its spire 160 feet high, a figure mentioned in the official guide as if height alone conferred merit.

The church was consecrated in 1903, completed in 1925, and is from a school of ecclesiastical architecture I can only describe as Neo-Devout, a school best exemplified by the sunken grotto outside the front door. I stopped there the next morning to watch a packed requiem mass, with incense and all the trimmings, and wondered idly whose funeral in Roscommon could pull so large a crowd. Immediately after the consecration, I sidled through the door, force of habit, last in, first out. It was market day in the center of town—not so much a square as a drunken triangle. The local merchants had set up stalls outside the Bank of Ireland, a building with a checkered history; it was formerly a Catholic church and before that a courthouse, Mammon having supplanted both God and Justice. Next to it a fortress of solid stone, once the county jail and scene of all Roscommon's public hangings. Centuries ago, the hangman was a woman, known only as "Lady Betty"; she was a convicted murderess whose death sentence was commuted on the condition she carry out the executioner's job without reward or recompense; all things considered, not a bad bargain. Would she, I wondered, now be called a hangperson? Down the street a whitewashed funeral parlor. "O'Shea Undertaker," read the sign over the door; in the window, another, smaller sign: "Antiques—Up the hill & turn right."

Back at Sacred Heart, another packed funeral mass. It took a moment before I realized it was the same casket in the center aisle, the same family of mourners in the front pews. Obviously a local personage to merit funeral masses back to back. There was a young priest standing at the back of the church, as if counting the house. "Excuse me, Father," I whispered tentatively.

"Father Ned," he corrected. He was scarcely twenty-five, fair-haired, with eyebrows so bleached by the sun they seemed invisible at first, as if they had disappeared into his skull. There was a pen poking importantly from the pocket of his ill-fitting black suit, the middle button missing, the other two buttoned up. He was wearing sandals and white socks.

"Well, then, I was just wondering, Father Ned . . ."

"Father Ned Corcoran . . ."

"Of course . . ."

"From Elphin . . ."

"Really." I was getting a bio. Ask him the time, he would tell me how to make a watch. "I was just wondering about the . . ." I tried to think of a phrase to describe the deceased with the proper respect. Corpse? Body? Stiff? Master of ceremonies? In the end I just waved toward the casket. "He must have been a distinguished member of the community."

"She . . ."

"Oh."

"Pat Curtin's ma."

"I see."

"Hanoria Dufficy that was. Ninety-eight, if she was a day."

"Ah . . ."

"The whole town was pulling for her to make a hundred years young."

"Of course."

"Tough as an old boot, she was." He leaned over so that he might speak into my ear. "And just as mean, if truth be told."

"Really?"

Heavy nodding. "I gave her the last rites myself, must be six times in all. She had an attack of gas and she'd say, 'Get me Father Ned.' Never the pastor."

There had to be a story in that, and I knew Father Ned was going to tell me what it was. "There was some bad blood between them." Once again he whispered into my ear. "Pat."

I had lost track. "Pat?"

"Pat Curtin."

"Of course." The son of the deceased.

"He got married in the C of I." The Church of Ireland. "It caused a rupture between Mrs. Curtin and the pastor. He said it was hellfire for Pat."

"That would do it."

"Which is why she always said, 'Get me Father Ned.' But he's saying the mass, you notice, the pastor."

"Forgive and forget," I said.

"Ashes to ashes and all that," Father Ned said. "You must be a friend of Pat's?"

I allowed as I did not know Pat Curtin.

"He's in America. I thought you might know him. He lives in the city of Denver. In the state of Colorado. It's a grand city, I'm told."

"It is that." I had changed planes there twice, my only two trips to Denver.

"Couldn't make it for the funeral. It's a long way, I suppose. He was over here in '86. Saw her then. It was the first, no, the second, time I gave her the last rites. It would be grand if you could tell him what a swell turnout she had, his ma."

I said if I ever ran into Pat Curtin I most certainly would. Then I added that I did think it unusual for someone, even Hanoria Dufficy Curtin, to have two funeral masses, one right after the other.

"Ah," said Father Ned, "there wasn't that much doing today anyway."

• •

STROKESTOWN IS a few miles north of Roscommon, a village
with a population of only seven hundred. I drove there later
that same morning, with a great sense of nervous anticipation,
Billy Burns's great-grandson returning home, Sir Bountiful
ready to bestow the warmth of his presence as if it were a
benediction. Before leaving New York, I had telephoned the
chancery of the diocese of Elphin, to which the parish of
Strokestown was subject, in order to get the name of the current pastor, whose good offices I thought I would need in
finding Poppa's baptismal record. In my heart of hearts, I
harbored another, equally sentimental (and equally specious)
notion: the pastor and I would become fast friends, who
would argue the existence of God over a wee dram, he tolerant
of my skepticism, I marveling at the strength of his faith.
I must have been out of my mind; the man who would believe
that would also believe in elves, leprechauns and four-leaf
clovers.

By coincidence the priest who answered the phone in the
chancery had once been a curate in Strokestown and was,
moreover, associated with the County Roscommon Historical
Society. His name was Beirne, and I suggested jocularly—
jocularity had become my form of discourse with anyone Irish,
even to the point of assuming a small brogue ("Jay-sus," I
had grown fond of saying)—that his Beirne and my Burns
might have one time been related, Beirne being the root from
which Burns was corrupted, Beirne also being one of the ten
most common names in Ireland. Father Beirne recommended
that I contact St. John's Heritage Center, a genealogical society in Strokestown, which was in the process of indexing all

parish records in Roscommon. In time I received a genealogical research form from the Heritage Center, filled it out with all the information I had available, however suspect I thought some of it was, and returned it with a check for thirty dollars to cover the cost of any research undertaken. My reference number was 87/176. I recited the number over and over: eight seven slash one seven six—Billy Burns's great-grandson. Sweet Jay-sus.

Strokestown is laid out along a broad avenue leading to the gated archway and demesne of Strokestown Park House, the graceful neo-Palladian home of the Mahon family, built on land given Nicholas Mahon by England's Charles II after the Restoration, for his service to the House of Stuart during the Civil Wars. The town's impressive main thoroughfare— Church Street—was designed, in the early 1800s, to the specifications of Maurice Mahon, who insisted that it be the widest street in Europe, an extraordinary pretension for a tiny market town in the middle of the vast Serbonian bog. Maurice Mahon razed every house, every pigpen, every structure that might have interfered with his plan and sight line, and flanked the cleared avenue on either side with the neat white row houses he built for his estate managers. Even today Church Street is still said to be one-half inch wider than O'Connell Street in Dublin.

St. John's Heritage Center is located at the west end of Church Street, in the deconsecrated Church of Ireland church that gives the avenue its name. Attributed to the architect Sir John Nash, the building is unusual in that the nave is an octagon rather than a rectangle, with a high beamed wooden ceiling, the eight massive composite beams converging into a central wheel-like design. St. John's was dedicated in 1820 and continued as a Protestant place of worship until 1977, when diminishing membership forced the Church of Ireland to order its closure and ultimate deconsecration. The building was ultimately acquired by the Strokestown Development Association, and in 1983, after renovation and restoration, it reopened as the Heritage Center.

The Heritage Center was empty except for the pert and compact young woman at the research desk. She was wearing a Swatch watch and white slacks and a green and white striped sweatshirt with a drawing of four military men on the front. "The City Marines," the logo on the sweater said. I gave her my name and said I had come to inquire about Dominick Francis Burns—reference number eight seven slash one seven six. Ah, yes, she said. It was as if she had been waiting for me to arrive. She had the genealogical research form I had filled out right there on her desk. Unfortunately, she said, she had been unable to uncover any information about Poppa, his parents or his siblings. There were no baptismal certificates, no marriage records. I was, of course, free to check through the records myself.

All the marriages and baptisms in Strokestown parish from 1830 to 1899 had been collected and collated into a central reference registry, with a cross-reference to the original document in the church where the information was found. From 1825 to 1866, the parish priest in Strokestown was Father Michael McDermott, his curates during those forty-one years Father Curley, Father Morris, Father Moran and Father Connolly. There was a note in the registry's foreword: "Variations in parents' names on the entries may be explained as error on the part of the priests at the time. Many of the baptisms do not seem to have been registered until long after the actual event. This may have resulted in a few mistakes being made when they were finally entered." The caveat seemed an admission that Father McDermott and his curates were perhaps only a little better educated than their parishioners. Another note urged that allowances be made for phonetic misspellings: "Behan=Boghan=Bohannon" was one example given; "Bosket=Bosquet=Bosquett=Bosquette" a second; "Carens =Kearns" a third.

From 1830 to 1899, according to the registry, there was only one Burns baptized in Strokestown and its outlying parishes, Mary Burns, born November 11, 1859, the daughter of Augustus and Margaret (Carney) Burns. In that same period, there were 122 baptisms recorded of children with some phonetic corruption of the name Beirne—Byrne, Birne, Beirn, Beryne, Bereen—but not a single Dominick in any of the variations. I considered the possibilities: either Billy Burns's son had not been born in Strokestown, or his baptism was never registered, or his name was not Dominick Francis Burns. In a way, I felt vaguely relieved. The mick from the hill would not have to worry how he would react to Cousin Malachy or Aunt Eileen. I travel easier without the baggage of history, and all a history's social and genetic freight. In the visitors' book, right after the couple from California who had written, "Well worth the price of admission," I wrote: "Keep up the good work."

OF COURSE before I left Strokestown I felt it incumbent to see how the landlord class had lived in the manor house at the opposite end of Church Street. It could not be said that any birth of the Mahons of Strokestown Park ever went unregistered. For supporting Irish union with England at the turn of the nineteenth century, George III granted Maurice

Mahon the title Baron Hartland. The Hartland title did not survive long, but the Mahons were nothing if not upwardly mobile. A later Mahon married into the distinctly more grand Pakenham family—Pakenham being the family name of the Earls of Longford. This union gave the Mahons a tenuous connection to the Duke of Wellington, as the Great Duke's wife was Kitty Pakenham. The Mahons rewarded themselves for their new eminence by changing their family name to Pakenham-Mahon, an affectation viewed with a certain wry disdain by their Longford relatives by marriage.

This I happened to learn while having dinner in London, shortly after I left Ireland, with the biographer-historian Antonia Fraser, whose father is Lord Longford and who herself was born Antonia Pakenham. When I asked her about the Pakenham-Mahons, she said that according to family lore an earlier Mahon had been manservant to the Longford earl of his day. After a lifetime of service, the retainer was preparing to retire. A retirement gratuity seemed to be in order, and the earl asked his man if there was any special favor he might grant. To which the servant replied that with his lordship's kind permission he would like to change his name to Pakenham-Mahon. Precise and careful historian that she is, Antonia Fraser said that the story was of course apocryphal, but that it has been passed from generation to generation does seem to indicate the low esteem in which the Pakenhams held the parvenu Pakenham-Mahons.

I tell the history of the Mahons in some detail only because Strokestown Park made me once again aware of that class resentment that still seems to bubble within me like an incubating virus. Beneath the house there was a system of tunnels through which servants could scurry from one wing to another without being seen by family members. A gallery in the kitchen allowed the lady of the house of observe what was happening below without ever having to be contaminated by physical contact with the staff; every Monday morning menus were dropped from the gallery with instructions for the week's meals. Outside the gate, there were no menus, no meals, only the Famine and starvation. On a desk in the library, there is a letter dated 18 April 1846, describing one James Killian of North Yard: ". . . starving all this year—has not a potatoe to eat when he goes home." Roscommon was particularly hard hit; in October 1846, a constabulary report stated that 7,500 people in the county were subsisting on boiled cabbage leaves once every forty-eight hours.

Strokestown Park had by then passed to Major Denis Mahon, a Protestant and an officer in the 9th Lancers, who had inherited the property from a lunatic uncle. Even before the onset of the Famine, the estate had been terribly mismanaged by the agents of the mad uncle; it was overtenanted and undercultivated, with rents three years in arrears. Then the potato crop failed. An officer used to a Lancers' mess and menus dropped from a gallery is not always the most compassionate of landlords. Compassion could only follow if the property was soundly managed, the free trader's definition of compassion being a plot of land so effectively tilled that it provided both rent for the landlord and food for the tenant. Toward this end, Denis Mahon offered his tenants an alternative—those who could not pay their rents would be either evicted or, at his expense, offered passage to Canada on two ships he had chartered. Pay or go—it was a hard man's hard bargain. Most tenants refused either to pay or to go, and of these over three thousand were evicted, a figure that included, according to the Bishop of Elphin, eighty-four widows. The 810 tenants who opted for Canada did not even fare as well.

On one ship, 268 passengers died at sea before the vessel dropped anchor in Quebec.

At home Denis Mahon was called a tyrant, from the pulpit, "worse than Cromwell." Rumors multiplied that he had chartered "coffin ships" for the voyage to Canada, one of which was said to have foundered with the loss of all aboard. The rumors about the ship's sinking were false, but the preemptive choices offered by Denis Mason, however in keeping they were with the principles of free trade, had poisoned the ground. Early in November 1847, Major Mahon was assassinated while driving from Roscommon in an open carriage. "The exultation of the country people . . . was general and undisguised," read a report from a Roscommon civil servant. "As soon as it was dark . . . signal was given of the deed having been perpetrated by lighting straw on some of the hills in the neighborhood of Strokestown, and on the following evening, when the people were better prepared, bonfires were seen on the hills for many miles in extent."

I sat in the library at Strokestown Park, staring out the window at green fields flecked with mustard. There was a Chinese Chippendale bookcase filled mainly with books on the fundamentals of bridge, and on the desk, *Poker—A Game of Skill*. I wondered if any Burns or Beirne or Beirn or Byrne or Birne or Bereen or Beryne—a relative—had been evicted by Major Mahon, or given passage on a coffin ship. I wondered if I would have lit a bonfire on hearing of his death. Probably not. The habit of caution is too strong.

I would have taken notes.

For future reference.

Know thyself.

To thine own self be true.

With a bundle on my shoulder
Sure there's no man could be bolder
I'm leaving dear old Ireland without warning.
For I've lately took the notion
To cross the briny ocean . . .

For home.

PART FIVE

XVII

It was not until the summer after my sister Virginia died that I finally learned why I could not find Poppa's baptismal record in Strokestown.

Ginny died in February.

Aunt Harriet had died the previous May.

Aunt Harriet's funeral mass was said at St. Peter Claver's, the same church in West Hartford where my mother's funeral was held, and my sister Harriet's. Aunt Harriet was ninety, almost ninety-one at her death. Grover Cleveland was president when she was born, Queen Victoria still a year short of her diamond jubilee. Aunt Harriet's lifetime spanned seventeen presidencies, a lifetime so long that a game of Trivial Pursuit could be played by trying to match the names of forgotten vice-presidents with the presidents they served— Charles Warren Fairbanks and Adlai E. Stevenson and Thomas Marshall and Garret Hobart and James Sherman. On her ninetieth birthday, incapacitated by a series of strokes and confined to an old persons' home, she received a card from Nancy and Ronald Reagan, a form greeting that the President sent when the White House was informed that a ninetieth birthday was coming up.

She was born Harriet Harrison Burns, but the day my brother Dick was born in 1924, she in effect lost that identity and became Aunt Harriet, and she was Aunt Harriet for the last sixty-three years of her life, Aunt Harriet to her six nieces and nephews, Aunt Harriet to her grand- and great-grand-nieces and nephews, Aunt Harriet to everyone with whom she came into contact, her friends, and our friends, and the friends of all those grand- and great-grand- nieces and nephews, never Harriet or Miss Burns, always Aunt Harriet. A writer friend of mine, a laicized Maryknoll priest and an exegete of the Catholic Church in its time of contemporary turmoil, once sent her a copy of a book he had written, inscribed, even though they had never met, "To Aunt Harriet . . ." Why, she asked me coyly, does he call me that? "Because," he replied, and I reported to her, "everyone has an Aunt Harriet, or should have."

She was a spinster, from a generation in which that word was a job description, a woman of virtue who did not question the idea of service to the family as an obligation to be endured. Twice in her life, she was called to active duty, and however much she might have resented being drafted, twice she responded. The first time was in the mid-1920s when, unexpectedly, her mother died. Immediately Poppa needed someone to run his household. There was only one choice: my mother, married and pregnant with her first child, was of course deferred. Aunt Harriet was not yet thirty, and though not of original bent, natively intelligent; and I think she realized that by taking on this task she would effectively be precluded from leading a life of her own, a life of independence either with or without husband and family, a life that, with Poppa's considerable wealth, she could easily have subsidized. Thenceforward, her life would be dedicated to Poppa, in his sixties, in vigorous health, a job that likely would see her into menopause and beyond, with possibilities fading and finally vanishing. Her response was to declare a vocation and enter the convent as a postulant, I suspect to avoid the world she saw closing in around her. She was a nun for less than a year. My surmise is that when she discovered the convent to be just another kind of institutional obligation, offering less freedom even than keeping her father's house, she left. She tended to Poppa until he died.

In the family, Aunt Harriet's brief tenure as a nun was never discussed. My mother would sometimes allude to it obliquely, but when pressed for further details would change the subject; I never knew Aunt Harriet even to allude to it. That year was the dark hole in her life, the source after she died of endless idle and often lurid family speculation. When we were children, we would wonder if she had shaved her head, as we were told nuns did, and it was an article of faith among us that when she bathed, she kept herself in some way covered, as nuns were not supposed to see their nakedness. "You have just been kissed by a virgin," her cousin Marjorie once cooed when Aunt Harriet planted a kiss on the brow of one of her nephews as he left the house. Aunt Harriet, nearing fifty, was stung to tears. Only Marjorie would dare talk in that risqué way, because she was, in the eyes of the Church, a fallen woman, having been divorced, and then remarried, to a divorced man. "Virgin" was the kind of word only a divorcée who smoked would say. The dirty thoughts that Marjorie conjured up, the wantonness that "divorcée" suggested.

• •

THE SECOND TIME Aunt Harriet answered the spinster's call to family duty was in 1946, right after my father died. With Poppa's death, she had for the first time staked out a life of her own, living first in the house where she grew up—Poppa's house—and then in a small apartment, attended by a bossy maid named Nellie. One morning in 1946, two days after my fourteenth birthday, I kissed my father goodbye and left for school. Shortly after my departure, as my father was dressing for the hospital and the operations he was scheduled to perform, his aorta burst. When I returned home that afternoon, I saw oxygen tanks on the back porch. I could not make it inside the door; it had to be Dad. My four older siblings were summoned from college and school, and Stephen and I farmed out for the night to friends of the family.

I had always had a cheeky relationship with my father. I inherited his volatile temper, which he vented both at home and in the operating room; at the hospital he had been known to fire interns and nurses in the midst of surgery if he felt they did not measure up to his standards. At home my older brothers and sisters had stretched his rules as far as they could be stretched, with the result that I was allowed to get away with far more than they ever had. I called myself "Dad's favorite son," and it was a mark of how much my father had mellowed that this cheekiness made him roar with laughter. I went to bed that night with the dull certainty that Dad's favorite son would soon be without a dad.

In the morning, Stephen and I were sent to school, assured by our hosts that everything would be all right. I was in study hall when through a window I saw a blue convertible Oldsmobile drive onto the school grounds. The car belonged to my mother's closest friend, a widow she had known since childhood, and when I saw her get out of the car and head for the administration building, I knew that my father had died, and that there was nothing to do except wait for the summons to the headmaster's office.

After the funeral, Aunt Harriet moved from her apartment into my mother's house. In effect, she became, especially to Stephen and me, who were so much younger than the others, a surrogate father. She was there. She provided. She was the adjutant to my mother's field marshal, the person against whom my mother often took out the considerable frustrations of being a widow. It was a thankless task, with no primary responsibility, but perhaps because of this Aunt Harriet had, I think, a more fierce sense of family than any of us. In the turbulent 1960s, when one of her grand-nephews, to the dismay of his parents, was preaching revolution and threatening to burn Harvard to the ground, I told him that if he ever blew up the Pentagon, Aunt Harriet would be the only one of his relatives to give him the money to leave the country. "Because she approved?" he asked incredulously. "No," I said, "because you're family."

She was the product of her age and time, and of the social stratification implicit in both. Hers was a world of ethnic codes, the particularity of "the" and "they" and "those people" always being used to describe the intolerable other. "We don't have Mexicans in Hartford," she told our Mexican baby-sitter once when we were visiting with our daughter. "We have the Puerto Ricans." Protestants were no less suspect. I would often rile her by saying the only reason she did not attend my wedding in California was because I married an Episcopalian. In time she became close to my wife, but the family always came first. "Will your book sell more than hers?" she asked when a novel of mine was published six months after one of Joan's. She also wanted to know if I sold more than Larry Collins, another Hartford writer, a contemporary of mine whose mother she saw at mass at St. Peter Claver's, and with whom I suspect she exchanged sales figures, to my disadvantage, unless she lied.

She was nearly eighty when my mother died, and a merciful God might have seen fit to take her soon after, but she lived another twelve years, alone, in failing health, only her power to exasperate, even to infuriate, undiminished. I talked to her every week from California, as I had with my mother, and each Christmas I arranged for her to be sent a weekly bouquet of spring flowers every Friday during the bleak winter months of January and February. Twice in those years, she was in the hospital when I returned to Hartford, and in a Demerol haze she would sometimes muse, in the most labyrinthine way, about paths not taken. There was nothing specific in what she said; I could only infer choices long ago made that, if she had been given the opportunity to relive her life, she might perhaps reconsider. On one of my visits in those last painful years, I took her to confession. I waited in the car outside the church. Confession seemed to take forever, especially for someone so innocent of sin. I finally went inside St. Peter Claver's to see if she was all right. The church was empty. And then from one of the confessional boxes I heard Aunt Harriet's voice, an almost plaintive cry: "But what of the sins of my past life?" I hastily left the church, a voyeur embarrassed that he had intruded on so private a moment.

After her stroke, she was unable to care for herself, unable to keep household help. Finally the family prevailed upon her to enter St. Mary's Home in West Hartford. While I was glad to see her when I was in the East, I hated going to St.

Mary's, hated passing through the phalanx of octo- and nona-
genarians parked in their wheelchairs in the corridor outside
her room, staring vacantly into space, a nightmare vision of
my own old age. She had trouble walking, and while her
speech more or less returned, she would often begin to weep
in midsentence. I think she must have known her physical
condition was such that she could never return to the house
where she and my mother had lived for so many years, but
as long as it was still in her hands she could nourish the de-
lusion that one day she would leave St. Mary's, and go home.

It was not to be. In legal terms, Aunt Harriet became, although still alive, "Estate of Harriet H. Burns," appraised
and organized, room by room, into "8 carved Hepplewhite
mahogany chairs" and "Coalport 'Kings Plate' china service
for twelve" and "Repro Victorian loveseat, blue brocade" and
"Light blue upholstered settee, soiled." The house was sold,
the belongings apportioned to the surviving children and
grandchildren. There is something so metaphorical and final
in the act of dividing up the possessions a family has accumu-
lated over several lifetimes and more generations; for the first
time I thought there might be a good argument for primo-
geniture. It was not that the furniture and china and crystal
and silver and linens had great worth; it was just that each
piece, each object, had a private history, a special meaning for
one or the other of us. For a family, the process of apportion-
ment is like psychoanalysis or the confessional box; long-buried
resentments surface, old hurts and forgotten slights. In the
end, a lawyer drew up the order of selection; his ground rules
were worthy of Solomon:

The order of selection will be determined as follows: each of
you is requested to pick a number from one to ninety-nine

and advise me of it by return mail; the person whose number is closest to the first two numbers of the Connecticut Daily Lottery on Tuesday, October 7, will have first pick, and so forth. . . . If the first person who selects property picks an item in an amount worth $1,400, the second person will be entitled to pick as many items as he or she wishes up to $1,400 in value. The third person would then have the right to choose property in the amount equal to the value selected by the person who preceded him or her and so forth until all items have been selected. In this way, each family unit will have an opportunity to select property, in turn and essentially of equal value.

The Connecticut State Lottery: God, if there is one, must have a sense of humor.

WHEN MY DAUGHTER was a child, she would often have night-mares about death. In these terrifying dreams, death was not an abstraction, but a person she called "the Broken Man." If the Broken Man comes, she would sob, I'll hold on to the fence so that he cannot get me. I thought of these nightmares often as Aunt Harriet drifted toward death. Life seemed to be the fence to which she clung in terror, trying to stave off the grasping fingers of the Broken Man. The last time I saw her, she was in the hospital, in and out of a coma, in and out of delirium. She clung to my finger the way a child does, her eyes unseeing, never focusing on where I was standing. "Father, forgive me for my sins," she suddenly screamed, and then: "Liars." It was not clear who the liars were, nor did I want to know.

The day before her funeral, I walked through the streets of Frog Hollow, where Poppa had prevailed and where she and my mother were born. It occurred to me that fashionable suburbs are never called Frog Hollow, and ghettos only rarely Brentwood Park. Gentrification had not come to the area. What had once been an Irish ghetto was now a Puerto Rican ghetto. "Ropa Para Toda la Familia," a faded gilt sign in a shopwindow said. "Vestidas de las Comuniones Primeras." Poppa's grocery store was still standing, reincarnated as a storefront office for a neighborhood service organization dedicated to finding jobs and ridding the area of prostitution and porno theaters. Down the street, at Immaculate Conception Church, only a side door was open, an attempt at crime prevention. Inside I picked up a church circular giving the hours for Misas, Confesiones, Bautismos; the assistant pastor, Father James Aherne, was identified as "Padre Jaimito."

My last stop was the Dominick F. Burns School. A few months after Poppa's death, the board of education had renamed the Lawrence Street School after him. According to the *Hartford Courant*, the Dominick F. Burns School is today "a melting pot and mini–United Nations," where students "converse in more than a score of foreign tongues." Of course the subtext of that boosterism is that Frog Hollow is still a redlined area, as multilingualism remained not much in evidence in the Yank enclaves of West Hartford or Farmington. I had never been to the Burns School before, and it is not a place a visitor simply walks into. He rings a bell, identifies himself, then is granted admission. In the office, a secretary was on the telephone: "He punched a kid out, then took off." To a teacher she explained: "Hector, Alfredo's on the rampage again." Back into the telephone: "The police are on the way, what else can I tell you." I had the sense that Poppa might have found this school named after him a mixed blessing. Finally I was able to introduce myself as the grandson of Dominick F. Burns. "Oh, I saw in the paper his daughter just died," the secretary said.

In death as in life, she was always D. F. Burns's daughter, or Aunt Harriet, never Harriet Harrison Burns.

VIRGINIA DIED nine months later, of cancer.

XVIII

As it happened, Poppa nearly emigrated not to Hartford but to Buenos Aires.

He was born not in Strokestown but nearby, in Tubberpatrick.

His name was not Burns, but O'Beirne.

His mother's maiden name was Elizabeth O'Beirne; when she married his father, William O'Beirne, she became Elizabeth O'Beirne O'Beirne. Elizabeth O'Beirne O'Beirne died from complications of giving birth to Poppa, her ninth child. After a suitable period of mourning, William O'Beirne married a widow, Eliza O'Beirne Cummings, who with their marriage became Eliza O'Beirne O'Beirne. According to family legend, William O'Beirne said that having had such good luck with one woman of that name, he decided to try marriage again with another.

For this information, I am indebted to an octogenarian first cousin once removed, Elizabeth Burns, daughter of Poppa's older brother William, with whom, in 1869, when he was twelve and William fourteen, he had journeyed from Strokes-town to Hartford. It was to Elizabeth Burns, a contemporary of Aunt Harriet's whom I scarcely knew, that I was led on my return from Ireland. She was, I was told, the unofficial historian and genealogist of the Burns family. Her response to my letter was so breezy, direct and indefatigable that it does not bear paraphrasing. First about Aunt Harriet:

> Obviously Harriet's life led her down a path which was completely different than mine. Hence, my visits to St. Mary's to see her have always been a source of concern for me in that I was afraid you, your brothers and Virginia might feel I was trying to "horn in," so to speak. Frankly those visits were the outgrowth of making a strictly courtesy call after her transfer to St. Mary's and discovering, much to my surprise, that Harriet was just plain lonesome. Unless—or until—you live with what I call the "over 90 set" (the older mentally alert but physically incapacitated individuals) for 24 hours a day, 7 days a week, 365 days in the year, you will never realize how important visitors from the outside world can be. That combination explains why the one-shot courtesy call became weekly visits.

And then to Ireland, about Poppa's father, her grandfather, my great-grandfather, William O'Beirne, born in 1820:

> My grandfather was considered fairly well off financially because he owned his own farm. That does not sound like much of a deal until you stop to consider that in that day and age a very high percentage (in fact the bulk) of Irish farms were owned by the English gentry and run by the Irish as tenant farmers. Why my grandfather decided to leave Ireland, in spite of the fact he owned his own farm, I'll never know, but

when it came to leaving Ireland it was a tossup as to whether they would come to the USA or go to Buenos Aires, where one of my grandfather's relatives (I thought it was an uncle, my sister Mary said it was Grandpa's brother) had settled. In the end Hartford won for the following reasons:

1. Grandma Burns lived in Hartford while she was married to Mr. Cummings (her first husband contracted a terminal illness—I think TB—and he decided to return to Ireland to die; that is how Grandma ended up in Ireland as a widow).

2. Grandma not only knew this area [Hartford] herself but she had a relative here who could, would, and did obtain living quarters for the family and buy the necessary furniture for same so that when Grandpa and his gang arrived in the USA they had a home ready for them to move into. I often have wondered what my life would have been like if my grandfather decided to settle in Buenos Aires instead of Hartford.

Amen.

A couple of more points regarding your great-grandfather. He is responsible for the change of the name from O'Beirne to Burns. Frankly, he decided to drop the "O" off somewhere in the Atlantic Ocean, but that was as far as he intended to go. However, the immigration officer could not understand his pronunciation (his sisters told me his brogue was so strong even "Burns" sounded like "Barns"), so when the immigration guy, after several tries, finally asked Grandpa if his name was spelled B-u-r-n-s, he agreed like it was. I never knew Grandpa Burns [who died in 1891] but I wish I had. He must have been quite a guy. Not known for his patience, but with it all a quick, intelligent man. I guess if I had a wife and six children waiting for me to clear through customs, and the man I was talking to could not understand me, I'd agree to anything, just to get by that checkpoint.

Incidentally, Grandpa Burns got a job in Colt's Willow Works. Bet you didn't know Samuel Colt, famous for his invention of the revolver, also had a factory which made furniture. Grandpa was the office manager, and when the Colt factory complex caught fire on night, Grandpa went in and saved his records. He was badly burned in the process but Mrs. Colt (she was the official owner of the Willow Works) was so grateful she paid his medical bills and continued his salary for a long time. I suspect the mathematical aptitude which runs through the Burns family came from that source—they say he was a real sharp cookie with figures and I know my father and his brothers were no slouches when it came to calculations.

That closes the book on your great-grandfather.

For reasons not entirely clear, William O'Beirne left his sons William and Dominick—Poppa—behind in Strokestown with a relative when he, his wife and six other children sailed for America in 1867. Two years later, Poppa and William followed:

They sailed from Liverpool. However, when they got to Liverpool, there was a dock strike and the boat did not leave on schedule. They were literally stranded. All they had was their passage. No money for food and lodging. One of the dock hands took pity on them, brought them home with him and kept them at his house until the boat sailed, which I believe was about a week later. Neither my father or your grandfather obtained that gentleman's name or address so the poor guy was never officially thanked (or reimbursed). I understand my grandfather was not happy with his boys because of that omission, but after all it is understandable. It was the first

time they were ever away from home so they were not aware
of such niceties.

Elizabeth Burns was also able to provide a firsthand report
on Poppa's only trip back to Strokestown, a three-day visit in
1907, via a letter sent immediately after his departure to her
father, William, by a cousin, one Michael Beirne:

> Next day (Sunday) we went to Mass and immediately after
> went to Tubberpatrick accompanied by Mickey Kelly's son,
> John, of Boarfield. We passed on by Tubberpatrick House as
> far as the bridge, and then returned and went through the field
> until we stood on the track of the house in which he [Domi-
> nick] was born. It is now giving meadow. I could observe that
> he was filled with emotion and that unpleasant reflections
> were crowding quickly upon his memory.

Unpleasant reflections: why? I thought of that farm William O'Beirne had once owned, "now giving meadow," and
his precipitate decision to leave Ireland for either America or
the Argentine. Had the farm been lost? And if so, under what
circumstances? And again I wondered why Poppa and William, one ten, the other twelve, had been left behind in Ireland while everyone else in their immediate family set out
across the briny ocean. What had that two years been like?
Were they the source of the unpleasant reflections?
Michael Beirne continued:

> Now, William, I must give you my impressions about Domi-
> nick. Isn't he a surprising fellow? I could not believe that he
> was the man he really is. Everyone who met him is speaking
> in the highest terms of him, and no wonder. He is so level-
> headed, intelligent, courteous and straightforward, and at the
> same time as simple and pleasing as a child. As far as I could

learn from him he is possessed of a good deal of the world's wealth. Of coure I did not want to pry into his secrets, and he is not a man for boasting.

Poppa did possess a good deal of the world's wealth. And in the fullness of his health and wealth he never did return to Ireland.

XIX

ON THE SECOND Sunday in February, seventeen months after the angioplasty, seven months after the trip to Ireland, four months after a MUGA bicycle test—nineteen minutes of heavy-duty exercise stress: "excellent ex capacity," according to the diagnostic report ("A man ten years younger than you without your history doesn't do half that well, Chief," my cardiologist, Tim, said)—I went for my morning walk in the park. It was a time of contemplation: what to make of Poppa's failure ever to return to Ireland; what to make of the departure of William O'Beirne, landholder, from Roscommon; how to mine the material, hold it up to the light, make use of it, refract it against my own life as it is, as it was, as I would invent it; what to add to the mix and what to subtract from it; how to manage and manipulate it; control it, control being the ultimate power, CONTROL, C-O-N-T-R-O-L; and more immediately, how to end this goddamn book.

Since it was Sunday, there were no cars in the park and I took a different route, up the steep grade of Cedar Hill on the roadway behind the Metropolitan Museum, knees pumping, sweat pouring. And then the knees would not work, the breath would not come. I rested, hands on my knees, joggers to the left and to the right and in front and behind, just rest here until I catch my breath. Then: Why was I lying on the asphalt? I did not recall going down. Oh, shit, I must have blacked out. Two seconds, four, five—enough time anyway to slide from hands on my knees to stretched out on the road, like a deadbeat drunk, or a homeless person lying on a grate in front of Ralph Lauren's on Madison Avenue across the street from my apartment, a source of embarrassment to the joggers who looked away, pretended not to see, this deadbeat with black sweat pants, the word "PRINCETON" in white and orange stitched on the left leg, going back, going back, going back to Nassau Hall, no longer in control, CONTROL, C-O-N-T-R-O-L, the ultimate degradation.

"Are you all right?" A Samaritan, not a jogger, with a canvas backpack book bag.

"I think so." The breath was coming back. I was sitting now, brushing gravel from my sweats, hoping the joggers would think I had only taken a nasty fall, the perils of keeping fit. On my feet. The Samaritan said he would call a cab on one of the emergency phones. No: I'll just wait here for a moment, thanks, anyway. Off the road there was what appeared to be a reviewing stand, and I sat there for a few moments, taking in the Museum and the cold blue Sunday sky, taking stock, what to do, what next, I'd really hate to cancel dinner tonight, dinner out with an anchorman and a big-time agent and a sports czar and a political commentator, I'm breathing normally now, it's okay, A-OK, I won't even tell Joan, nor Tim, especially not Tim, I feel fit as a fiddle now. And fit as a fiddle I walked home. In the distance I saw Joan walking the big, shaggy, pain-in-the-ass Bouvier down another path, his post-prandial mark and dump. And I knew I would tell her: we had not stayed married for twenty-five years by keeping secrets, however unpleasant, from one another.

I called Tim, I told Joan. We went to dinner with the anchorman, the big-time agent, the sports czar and the political commentator. My mind was elsewhere.

Tim's test the next day replicated the exercise conditions in the park. Another blackout. You've got a problem, Chief, Tim said. The symptoms indicate aortic stenosis, Tim said. Aggressive diagnostics, Tim said, and I suspect some surgery. Open-heart surgery. To replace the aortic valve, the valve that had not even been much of a factor in the earlier disagreeable episode. And as long as they're in there, Tim said, a bypass, and then you're fit as a fiddle and ready for love.

O.K.

"I think I know how to end this book now," I said to my wife on the walk home from Tim's. I knew I did not have to spell it out to her.

"Terrific," she said, the novelist in her taking precedence over the wife who knew her husband too well ever to express the concern she felt, the husband who was so volatile except in times of crisis.

"It's a hell of an ending," I said, and what I meant was that a writer's life is his only real capital, his and his alone to invest, and to imagine, and to reimagine, even unto this.

WELL, HELL, yes, it's what I do.

OPEN-HEART SURGERY was scheduled, but canceled the afternoon before it was to be performed. The angiogram had shown no aortic stenosis, but instead a coronary tree—a wonderful phrase, new to me, evoking spring—that would be the envy of men ten years younger, healthy men with no dubious cardiac history. I was, in fact, slightly disappointed, overcome, after having psyched myself up for surgery over a period of three weeks, by a sense of anticlimax. And riven by the question that carried with it a certain heightening of the existential dilemma: why had I passed out? I remembered a story I had been told about a political prisoner in South Africa. After nine years in prison, he was finally released, shortly before Christmas. It had been the custom in his prison for the political internees to pool their meager resources and bake themselves a Christmas chocolate cake. When the prisoner was released, his first feeling was one of resentment, that he would miss that year's cake.

WELL, HELL, yes. I would miss the cake.

Acknowledgments

I would like to thank David Stein, Stephen C. Berens and Francis Minot Weld. Had it not been for them, I do not think this book would have been written. I can only say that I am the son of a surgeon, and as doctors they remind me of my father. I can think of no higher praise.

Thanks also to Rose Fontaine and to Maria Ynez Camacho who made life so infinitely much easier. And to Barbara Cooke, Cathy McCarty Doyle and Rebecca Stowe: they ran the business, they talked to the Feds and to the insurance companies, they tracked down the odd fact in the obscure book, they bought me time.

And thanks to Lynn Nesbit, Morton L. Leavy, Jeffrey Berg and Gilbert Frank—generous with friendship, generous with advice and counsel, and so generous of spirit that they allow me to keep more than eighty percent of what they make for me.

And finally, thanks to Alice Mayhew. To those of us fortunate enough to have worked with her, the mere mention of her name is acknowledgment of what she means to any book with which she is associated.